Anita is leery of seeing too much of Regan Moore, but her six-year-old son, Tyler, has other plans.

Anita allowed Regan to step inside the apartment, then bent for Tyler to plant a kiss on her cheek. Tyler giggled. "Now you have the mark of the black lips."

A vision of her son's dark imprint on her cheek made her laugh. "And what's the mark supposed to mean?"

"Only the one who loves you can give it to you." Tyler beamed and stole a look at Regan.

How sweet. "Then I qualify, don't I?" Anita hugged him.

"Right. You're the best mom in the whole world, better than those silly old girls at school."

Before she had time to expound on the good qualities of little girls, Tyler added, "Mr. Regan, why don't you give Mom a kiss and see if it shows up black on her face?"

For yet another embarrassing moment, of which she'd had her share since meeting Regan, Anita didn't know whether to apologize or say nothing. And she refused to catch his gaze.

"I think I'll pass this time," Regan said hastily.

Thank you, Mr. Moore.

"Why?" Tyler stared up at the fire marshal.

Regan cleared his throat. "I don't think it works on the same person twice."

"Oh, okay." Tyler nodded thoughtfully. "Tell you what. Next time I'll let you kiss Mom, so it's fair."

DIANN MILLS draws the broken to wholeness in her writing. She lives in Houston, Texas, with her husband Dean. They have four adult sons. She wrote from the time she could hold a pencil, but not seriously until God made it clear that she should write for Him. After three years of serious writing, her first book *Rehoboth* won favorite Heartsong Presents historical for 1998. Other publishing credits include magazine articles and short stories, devotionals, poetry, and internal writing for her church. She is an active church choir member, leads a ladies' Bible study, and is a church librarian. Her Web site is *www.diannmills.com*.

Books by DiAnn Mills

HEARTSONG PRESENTS
HP291—Rehoboth
HP322—Country Charm
HP374—The Last Cotillion
HP394—Equestrian Charm
HP410—The Color of Love
HP441—Cassidy's Charm
HP450—Love in Pursuit
HP504—Mail-Order Husband

Don't miss out on any of our super romances. Write to us at the following address for information on our newest releases and club membership.

Heartsong Presents Readers' Service
PO Box 721
Uhrichsville, OH 44683

Or visit www.heartsongpresents.com

Licorice Kisses

DiAnn Mills

Heartsong Presents

To Sandy and Ted Galde. Many thanks for your help and encouragement.

A note from the author:
I love to hear from my readers! You may correspond with me by writing:

DiAnn Mills
Author Relations
PO Box 719
Uhrichsville, OH 44683

ISBN 1-58660-627-1

LICORICE KISSES

All scripture quotations, unless otherwise indicated, are taken from the HOLY BIBLE, NEW INTERNATIONAL VERSION ®. NIV ®. Copyright © 1973, 1978, 1984 by International Bible Society. Used by permission of Zondervan Publishing House. All rights reserved.

All of the characters and events in this book are fictitious. Any resemblance to actual persons, living or dead, or to actual events is purely coincidental.

Cover illustration by Kay Salem.

PRINTED IN THE U.S.A.

one

The Spirit of the Sovereign Lord is on me,
because the Lord has anointed me to preach good news
to the poor. He has sent me to bind up the brokenhearted,
to proclaim freedom for the captives and release
from darkness for the prisoners.
ISAIAH 61:1

Anita Todd glanced at her watch and realized she had less than an hour before her appointment with the fire marshal. Swirling around in her chair from an open file cabinet, she viewed the mound of paperwork on her laminated desk and knocked over a bottle of water. It sloshed across her mouse pad, soaked her notes, and dripped onto the blue-green carpet.

"Wonderful," she muttered as she snatched up a handful of tissues to soak it up, but they merely stuck to her fingers—obviously meant for noses not oceans of water. She reached for another, except the box teetered and fell into the small puddle.

"Oh, Mom, you made a mess," six-year-old Tyler said, nodding in a grown-up fashion. "I'll get the paper towels." His words echoed down the hallway as he raced to the kitchen of the newly constructed preschool and kindergarten building.

"Thanks," she called. At least the water had missed her computer keyboard and jeans.

Tyler quickly returned. "Here ya go. Do you want me to do it for you?" His chocolate-brown eyes revealed his concern.

"Hey, I'm fine." She offered a smile. "A little water never hurt anyone." She tore into the plastic wrapper of the paper towels and immediately sponged up the water.

"You nervous about the 'spection?" He studied her through nearly an inch of eyelashes just as his father used to do.

"I must be." She tossed the wet towels into the trash and shook her head. "Leave it to your mom to come down with a case of the 'clumsies' at the wrong time."

"When will the fire guy be here?" Tyler sat at a small table designed for children to construct interlocking building projects.

Anita smiled at her son and his miniature city complete with tiny people and vehicles. "He's not a fire guy, Sweetie, but a fire marshal for the city of Sweetwell. His job is to make sure the school is safe for the children, and he'll be here in about an hour." She took a long look at Tyler's work. "Say, you have a fine looking town here."

He beamed and added a tiny tire to a little truck. "Will his 'spection be a piece of cake?" With his front two teeth missing, "piece" sounded more like "peeth."

"I'm sure everything will be fine." She ruffled his thick hair. "Then I need to touch up some painting in the two-year-old room before we call it a day. One of the teachers accidentally scraped a wall when she was moving her desk."

"Do you need my help?"

"Oh, not this time, but thanks for asking." Heaven forbid if he took a paintbrush to one of these walls.

"Can we get a movie for tonight?" Tyler asked. The afternoon sunlight picked up a splattering of freckles across the bridge of his nose, reminding her of gold dust.

"I suppose, but let's find some from the church library. In fact, the library is open all afternoon. Why don't you and I head that way and see if you can select your movies while the fire marshal is visiting?"

Tyler agreed and immediately went to work picking up scattered building pieces and placing them in a container beside the small table.

She headed toward the kitchen to put away the paper towels

and take one last look at each schoolroom. A mixture of fresh wood and paint teased her nostrils. What preschool director wouldn't want a brand new facility?

Kindergarten and preschool classes were scheduled to begin the following Wednesday for Good Hope Christian Day School. So far, the deadlines and requirements had all been met. The representative from Oklahoma's Department of Human Services would be there on Monday for the state's final inspection, but she needed the fire marshal's signed approval today for all of the licensing requirements.

The files, she thought nervously. *I need to go through the files one more time to make sure everything is in order.*

The phone rang, and Anita rushed back to her desk. She grabbed the portable phone and realized the paper towels were still in her hand. *I'm losing it,* she thought. "Good Hope Christian Day School." Her voice rang with rehearsed pleasantness.

"Hi, Honey. Are you running crazy?"

"I think so, Mom." She smiled into the receiver, picturing her round, gray-haired mother sitting at the kitchen counter in between watching her "stories." Her mother kept saying she knew one day a TV network would come up with a Christian soap opera. Until then, she occasionally viewed the regular ones despite Anita's urging for her to read or take up a hobby during those viewing hours.

"Has the fire marshal been there yet?"

"No, but I'm about ready," Anita replied with a sigh.

"Why am I not convinced? I'm sure everything is in perfect shape."

Anita forced a laugh. "I've checked the files and reports a dozen times, but I'm still rattled."

"You'll do fine; just relax. I didn't call to keep you. I just wondered if you and Tyler would like dinner tonight."

"Oh, Mom, I'm beat. Thanks anyway, but I'd rather go home and crash."

"All right, and I certainly understand. Give my favorite grandson a hug for me, and if anything changes, give me a call."

"Thanks, Mom." Anita hung up the phone and considered how much she appreciated her mother. *Her favorite grandson. Tyler's her only grandson.*

She pulled the file containing all her inspections from the cabinet behind the desk and laid it near the phone. A twinge of anticipation raced through her body. She'd worked long and hard all summer to make sure the church's first state-licensed preschool and kindergarten would be ready for students next week.

New teachers, capable aides, curriculum, learning centers, supplies, books, music, and furniture were obtained according to specific standards and, of course, the church's budget. Earlier in the month, the staff attended a weeklong in-service program designed to not only prepare them for the children but also to equip them in new teaching methods, First Aid, and CPR training.

Although the fire marshal didn't need access to the staff and children's files, Anita opened the huge four-drawer file cabinet anyway. She knew those folders contained all the health and safety forms mandated by the state for the children plus complete files on the teachers regarding their education, previous teaching records, health, criminal background checks, letters of recommendation, church history, and statements of faith.

Last of all, she leafed through her own file as director. Copies of her credentials, recommendation letters, and her master's degree in elementary education with a minor in religion sat crisply in her file. She cringed at the piece of paper noting her minor. A lot of good biblical knowledge did for her life; nothing in those studies prepared her for widowhood or a son with recurring nightmares. Closing the file abruptly, Anita nudged the resentment from her mind to concentrate on what she needed to do now.

"I'm ready," Tyler said, pushing the small chair under the table. As if expecting her next comment, he tucked his T-shirt inside his navy shorts.

"Hmm, you look nice and neat," she said with an admiring glance.

A few moments later, the two walked across the church grounds to the library, which housed books, DVDs, videos, and music for children and adults.

Anita peered up at the huge, gray brick structure of Good Hope Church. She had attended there from childhood until, as a college senior, she had met Vince Todd, a recent law graduate. Within a year they were married and moved to Tulsa. The first few years were perfect, then it all fell apart.

She shook her head in an effort to dispel the painful memories. Despite her years of church attendance and Bible study, she failed to understand God's reason for taking Vince from her and Tyler.

When Good Hope needed a director for a new preschool and kindergarten program, Anita had applied for the position. Elation had consumed her when the preschool board accepted her application. She suspected her mother had a lot to do with it, but it didn't matter. The prospect of returning to her hometown and living close to her mother seemed like a dream come true.

Tyler opened the glass library doors for her, and the two stepped inside to greet the librarian, an attractive brunette.

"Hi, Denise. Do you mind if Tyler looks at books and picks out a movie or two? I'm expecting the fire marshal."

The librarian waved her hand as though swatting a pesky fly. "No problem. Take your time. Tyler and I will have a good visit."

"Thank you so much. You're a lifesaver." Anita hurried back to the school for one last look before the fire marshal's appointment.

A tall, sandy-haired man in a white shirt and blue khaki

pants stood waiting at the front door.

"Good afternoon." Anita waved.

The man turned, and her gaze flitted to a fire marshal insignia on his left shirt pocket. She read the name Regan Moore across a pin just below it. He'd arrived early and appeared clearly annoyed.

"I'm sorry to keep you waiting," Anita said cheerfully, inwardly scolding herself for wasting time at the library.

"I've already written you a note canceling our appointment." His grim mannerisms punctuated her nervousness.

"I believe our appointment is at two o'clock." Anita felt perspiration mount and slip down the side of her face. *It's only one-thirty!*

"Didn't my office tell you I would be a few minutes early?" he asked, and she noticed the coldness in his steely eyes.

"Yes, Sir, but I assumed about fifteen minutes early."

"Haven't you ever been told not to assume anything?" He reminded her of Tyler's snapping turtle.

"I'm sorry, Mr. Moore. I'm Mrs. Todd." She extended her hand, and he loosely grasped it. The scowl appeared permanently glued to his harsh features.

He handed her a white business card with black-and-red lettering—obviously his introduction. She examined it carefully, wondering if she should ask for identification, but thought better of it in view of his scrappy temperament.

"Since you're here, I'd like to see the school," Mr. Moore stated, his tone as crisp as his starched pants.

While Anita fumbled with the keys, she silently chided herself for not being in her office when he arrived. No doubt, her tardiness had placed him in a foul mood.

"Would you like me to show you through the school?" She attempted politeness while wondering how this man had earned his position as fire marshal. He certainly hadn't received the Mr. Congeniality award.

"I'd rather take my own tour," he replied, not once offering her eye contact. "I have a diagram of the building, so I'll inspect the rooms, make notes, and go over my findings with you when I'm finished."

All during the inspection, Anita sat at her desk fuming about the man's rudeness and worrying about what he might find, but she knew everything was in order. She couldn't attend to anything, and the longer she waited, the more apprehensive she became. After forty-five minutes, he called to her from the hallway.

"Mrs. Todd, can I see you a moment, please?"

Anita trembled, and she willed her body to stop. The tone of the fire marshal's voice sounded less than friendly.

Regan Moore stood writing on a form fastened securely to a clipboard. "I see you're licensed for one hundred and fifty children and the rooms have been assigned with the number of children permitted in each room along with the number of teachers and aides required to insure proper student-teacher ratios," he said stiffly, his nose glued to the form before him. "The emergency evacuation plans are clearly posted, and the kitchen is in order. Now, I need your electrical, gas, heating and air-conditioning, and health department inspections."

"Of course. They are on my desk, " Anita replied. *He has absolutely no tact.*

"You must enjoy children to consider this undertaking." He glanced into a preschool room.

At least he has one soft spot.

"Yes, they are very special little people."

He walked over to examine a home-living center, complete with child-size furniture and accessories. Mr. Moore touched a rocking chair and watched it sway back and forth.

"Do you have children?" she asked, hoping a mutual topic might smooth his crusty exterior.

His gaze flew to hers, and she saw something akin to pain.

"No," he said, rapidly moving toward the door. "I need to see those inspection reports."

She followed him to the front desk and watched him methodically examine the reports. Silence seemed to echo from the corners of the building.

"Everything appears to be fine," he finally said.

Anita breathed a sigh of relief. *Now, if he would simply sign the inspection report and leave.*

"However, there's one problem. Paint cans in the two-year-old room are not permitted. In fact, I can show you the page number and paragraph in your Department of—"

"I know about the regulations, Sir," Anita said, feeling her skin grow devoid of color. "And those cans won't be there after this afternoon. I have some touch-up painting to do before classes begin next Wednesday. One of the teachers accidentally scraped the walls when she rearranged furniture."

"Mrs. Todd, I'm sorry, really I am, but I cannot bend the rules to accommodate your plans. I make these inspections as if the children are in attendance. You have violated a very important law regarding fire safety. If you will give me your copy of the state's standards, I'll show you."

"I believe you." Anita felt defeated and miserable. As soon as the words escaped her mouth, she realized he heard her frustration.

"Paint is flammable and poisonous," he said a little more softly. "I know you wouldn't want a child hurt."

"I know the chemicals are dangerous, but the school hasn't opened yet," she replied as misery slowly consumed her.

Mr. Moore cleared his throat. "As I stated before, your plans cannot affect my findings. I'm sorry if this causes a problem with your opening day, but the children are my main concern. I will have to come back in order to give you a valid inspection."

Oh, no. This can't be happening. "But the Department of Human Services will be here Monday." Anita's hands hung limp at her side. "Please, the school needs the inspection to obtain our license."

He hesitated. "What time is your social worker scheduled to arrive?"

"Monday afternoon, one o'clock," Anita replied, ordering her heart to cease the furious pounding against her chest.

"All right, I'll be here at twelve." He snapped his pen back under the clipboard.

Regan Moore reminded her of one of her mother's familiar quotes: "If he didn't have such an ugly personality, he might be tolerable."

"What if I remove the paint cans from the building while you're here?" Anita asked, feeling the weight of everything going wrong.

"What good would that do?" Mr. Moore placed the clipboard under his arm as though he held some military report affecting world security. "You've already told me you need to finish painting. I couldn't sign the inspection knowing you might endanger the lives of innocent children. As long as the paint cans are on the premises, this building is a fire hazard. No, Mrs. Todd, I cannot do as you ask."

She realized it made little sense to argue with the city's fire marshal. He apparently never deviated from his rule book. She concluded Mr. Regan Moore had the state fire code memorized.

"Thank you for coming." She lifted her chin. "I'll have the painting completed and the cans removed by Monday morning."

She watched him leave in a fire engine red Jeep, complete with a roaring motor. His bumper sticker scraped her nerves: Fire Safety Isn't Just a Good Idea—It's the Law.

❧

Fire Safety Isn't Just a Good Idea—It's the Law. Regan had noted the slogan on his bumper sticker as he'd rounded his Jeep. *But I don't have to act inhuman about it.*

He stopped at the end of the private driveway of Good Hope School to turn onto the main road and palmed his fist on the steering wheel. He'd been a real jerk back there. A good man would turn around and apologize to Mrs. Todd. He couldn't change his report status, but he could show a bit of kindness.

Taking a deep breath, Regan decided to wait until Monday. With the mood he was in right now, he'd blow an apology.

৯৯

For several minutes, Anita paced the hallway, reliving every word and gesture of her encounter with the fire marshal. The intensity of her anger left her shouting at the walls and slamming a few doors. Anita knew she must calm down before walking over to get Tyler from the library.

Regan Moore had zilch in the way of people skills. Not only did he lack communication abilities, but he also had no concept of the hard work involved in preparing a school for opening day. How could anyone ever paint or remodel a building under his jurisdiction?

I would never make this school a dangerous place for children. The nerve of him! What a disgusting model of mankind.

Taking several deep breaths, she downed the rest of her warm bottle of water and made her way to the library.

"What's wrong?" Denise asked as soon as Anita approached her desk.

She had intended to say nothing about Mr. Moore's visit, but the question brought his insolence to the surface again. She thought better of revealing the entire incident, but she did indicate her dissatisfaction with his findings.

"I'm sorry he gave you such a bad time," Denise replied.

"Me too," Anita said. "Well, there's nothing I can do about it but prepare myself for Monday's return visit. I refuse to let this minor setback ruin my weekend."

"Exactly," Denise agreed with a sigh. "It will all work out. I know the fire marshal, and he's normally very pleasant."

Oh, great. Now I've opened my big mouth, and he'll probably find out about my exasperation with him. "I'm sure I overreacted," Anita added. "You know, a case of jitters with the school opening next week."

Denise smiled kindly and handed Anita the DVDs Tyler had selected. "I know you've worked very hard to put the school together. Parents are excited about the program, and teachers are looking forward to their classes."

Anita couldn't help but return the smile. "You are so sweet to encourage me. Thank you, and I appreciate your keeping an eye on Tyler."

Late afternoon shadows crept across the driveway of the school's parking lot by the time Anita and Tyler locked up and headed home. The phone had rung repeatedly all afternoon, and she hadn't done any of the painting.

"Mom, I'm sorry you had a bad day," Tyler stated as he clicked his seat belt in place and adjusted the shoulder harness.

"Oh, my, did you hear me talk about the fire marshal?" Guilt settled upon Anita worse than in the immediate aftermath of the fire marshal's ultimatum.

"Yeah, I did," Tyler replied. "He must have a problem."

She laughed at his imitation of her mother. "Don't you think another thing about it, and I'm sorry you heard me complain about him."

"No problem, Mom. Sometimes I have bad days."

She laughed again at his adult-sounding consolation and reached across the seat to take his hand. "So what do we do tonight, Bud, popcorn and movies?"

Tyler grinned. "Sure, Mom. We'll just party."

Once they reached home, Anita checked her phone recorder for messages.

"Hi, Honey, this is your mother. I forgot to remind you earlier today about the gentleman from church stopping by this evening to meet you and Tyler. He's the one from Big Brothers who offered to visit with our little man. Anyway, before he plans anything with Tyler, he wanted to meet you both. He told me he'd stop by around seven o'clock."

"Oh, great, Mom," Anita said under her breath. The thought of dealing with a man from church ground at her nerves.

She quickly shoved aside her thoughts. Tyler needed a man's attention, and her son would be thrilled at the prospect of a male spending quality time with him. After all, she couldn't argue with the credentials of a representative from church, especially one her mother recommended.

"Awesome!" Tyler shouted when she told him the news. "Wow, a Big Brother, just like Grandma promised." He grew even more excited when he learned the man planned to visit them during the evening. After gulping down his macaroni and cheese, he volunteered to help clear the table and load the dishwasher. He chatted on about what type of activities this new Big Brother might want to do with him. Anita listened and tried to emulate her son's enthusiasm.

She watched his eyes grow wide, talking about everything from soccer and movies to wild animal hunting in the jungles. Sometimes watching Tyler brought back sweet memories of Vince. Tyler had his father's eyes, nearly black curly hair, long legs, and talked in constant motion with his arms. Anita and Tyler were so caught up in the discussion about the Big Brother that when the doorbell rang, it startled them.

"I'll get it," Tyler said, scrambling to the door.

"Honey, I will," she replied. "If this is the man from Big Brothers, then I need to meet him first."

She opened the door to a man standing before her in jeans and a pullover shirt—Regan Moore, the city's fire marshal.

two

Regan Moore's mouth clearly stood agape. "You're Anita Todd?" he asked. "Director of Good Hope Christian Day School? Tyler Todd's mother?"

Anita struggled to hide her displeasure. The man had gotten the best of her once today, and she planned to emerge victorious in this round.

"Yes, can I help you?" She still held on to the front door. Had he discovered yet another violation of the fire code?

"Mrs. Gavanti gave me this address for a little boy and his mother whom I'm supposed to meet this evening." He pulled a piece of paper from his jeans pocket and confirmed why he'd interrupted her evening. "I didn't pay attention to the last name until now. Guess I should have."

"You're the big brother my mother arranged for Tyler?" Yielding to a surge of mixed emotions—anger, shock, and definitely disillusionment—Anita could no longer hide her dismay. What a role model for Tyler.

"Yeah, I'm afraid so." He looked as uncomfortable as she felt.

Tyler stepped from behind her and posed an infectious smile. She saw no alternative but to introduce the man. "Tyler, this is Mr. Moore, the man Grandma arranged to visit you."

Her son extended his right hand, his manners polished, just as she had taught him. "Hello, I'm Tyler Todd. Pleased to meet you."

"Pleased to meet you too. I'm Regan Moore." He shook her son's hand and smiled warmly, the first gesture of friendship she'd seen from him.

"Boy, my mom had a bad day with another guy named Mr. Moore."

"I'm sorry," he said, glancing at Anita with a furrowed brow.

She felt her face grow warm, and she dug her fingers into the palms of her hands. *Please, Tyler, don't say another word.*

"Yeah. She said his face would crack if he smiled, and he was in—in—intolerable. Isn't that right, Mom?" Tyler looked up at her as if for confirmation.

She took a deep breath and wished she could sink through the beige carpet of their second-floor apartment. "Tyler, we don't need to discuss this right now." She lifted her gaze to Mr. Moore, offering an apology, although he deserved to know how she felt about his earlier behavior.

"Aren't you gonna let him in?" Tyler asked with eagerness.

Trapped by my own son. "Of course," she managed, feigning a gracious attitude as she opened the door a fraction wider.

He nodded and stepped inside, easing past her cautiously.

"I intended to call you on Monday morning," he said quietly, reaching deep into his jeans pockets. "I do apologize for today, Mrs. Todd. I can explain."

She felt more awkward as the tension mounted between them. "It's over and done with. Why don't you sit with Tyler in the living room while I finish cleaning up the kitchen? You two can get to know each other."

The fire marshal followed the lively six year old, and shortly thereafter, Anita realized the TV had been turned off. Soon the sound of laughter filled the apartment, but Anita felt even more miffed at Mr. Moore's earlier treatment.

She took her time in rinsing dishes and placing them in the dishwasher. Normally she wiped off the sink and left the towel to dry, but tonight she scoured the stainless steel surface and polished the chrome until she could see herself. Unfortunately, she didn't feel as radiant as the shiny metal. Whirling about her, she elected to sweep the floor and check the laundry. While folding Tyler's soccer uniform, she felt someone watching her.

"I do owe you an explanation," a male voice said.

She looked up and swallowed hard. Her uneasiness seemed to devour her. No one should feel this way in their own home.

Without waiting for a response, he continued. "Just before I reached your school, my parents phoned me with some bad news. It doesn't excuse my nasty disposition, but it does give you a reason behind it."

She turned to offer her best manners, refusing to copy the inconsiderate behavior he had exhibited this afternoon.

He cleared his throat and leaned against the doorway. "Anyway, my grandmother passed away today, and the news hit me harder than I expected."

"Oh, I'm sorry," Anita said, genuinely sincere. *Why didn't he explain himself this afternoon?*

"Thank you, but I should have said something about her death this afternoon instead of taking it out on you."

"Most certainly. We could have postponed the inspection—"

"With Human Services scheduled for Monday?" he asked, reminding her again of their earlier unpleasantness.

Anita swallowed a sharp rebuttal, but then she remembered her tactless remarks after Vince's death. "I am sorry about your grandmother, and as long as you're able to be there at noon on Monday, I don't foresee a problem."

"Thanks for being so understanding," Mr. Moore said. "Doubt if I could be so forgiving in your shoes."

Anita noticed a dimple on his right cheek, but neither the boyish appeal nor his apology wiped away the memory of the afternoon. If he really regretted his rudeness, he could have handed her a signed fire inspection.

"I've already forgotten the matter." Anita firmly pushed away the tug on her conscience for lying and pulled one of Tyler's T-shirts from the dryer. "Please, don't let the afternoon interfere with this evening. Tyler has been very excited about your coming."

He paused in the kitchen while she folded clothes—more painstakingly than usual. "There's something else. Tyler invited me to watch a movie, but I wanted to check with you first."

Great. Now I have to endure you for another hour. "Of course, go ahead," Anita quickly responded, except she resented anyone other than her mother viewing movies with her son. She'd looked forward to spending tonight with Tyler—alone.

Mr. Moore turned to walk away but again hesitated. "Mrs. Todd, your mother indicated Tyler has an early morning soccer game. Do you mind if I attend?"

Possessiveness gripped her heart. Nursing her ruffled feelings, she wished Tyler's Big Brother was anyone but the fire marshal.

"It's early, eight o'clock." She hoped he slept in. "And it's at Bennet's Field, behind the park."

"I'll be there. . .and thank you again." With his features softened, he really didn't look so bad, but his display of temperament earlier caused her to raise questions about the Big Brother program. Fire flew from the pores of her skin each time she thought about the afternoon. Nothing, absolutely nothing, could excuse bad manners. After all, he had allowed his personal life to interfere with his profession. A true professional never permitted emotions to override good judgment.

She folded her arms across her chest as he disappeared into the living room. Anger flowed through her veins. This man had successfully intruded into her life twice today, and she didn't like it. He'd explained the circumstances surrounding their earlier meeting, but she wasn't ready to forgive or forget. Why had she agreed to such nonsense as Big Brothers?

With a deep breath, she once again admitted to herself that Tyler needed a male role model, but she felt certain Regan Moore didn't meet the qualifications.

Anita popped the corn and made a pitcher of lemonade.

Reluctantly, she joined the two in the living room, where they roared with laughter at the animated movie. The well-meaning fire marshal sat beside Tyler on her comfortable green leather sofa with his arm stretched across the back of it.

Mr. Moore had her spot.

She placed the snacks on the antique trunk that doubled as a coffee table and slid into a side chair—purchased for style and not comfort. With a little luck, he'd be bored soon and leave. Better yet, she might find another flaw in his character—serious enough to discourage a relationship between him and Tyler. Regan Moore needed to oversleep in the morning and miss the soccer game. That bit of concession would give her enormous satisfaction.

⋙

A rare chill met the morning's soccer game. The crisp air allowed the boys to expend extra energy. They shouted, raised high fives, and hollered their anticipated victory while their voices echoed for at least a mile. Anita had brought a huge thermos of ice water for Tyler, then pulled through a drive-through for a large black coffee for herself.

The boys practiced kicking and passing before the game, and Anita happily noted the fire marshal's failure to appear. More than once she saw Tyler look for him, and each time disappointment etched his round face. She felt guilty, not at all triumphant as she'd wanted.

The referee blew the whistle for the game to begin. The boys took their positions with Tyler defending the goal. She saw a smile spread across her son's face and knew Regan Moore must have arrived. Silently, Anita scolded her selfish attitude. She found reason after reason for her coldness to the man, but Tyler's well-being came first. The man had only expressed a desire to befriend a fatherless boy. Anita and Mr. Moore's professional relationship shouldn't get in the way. Wonderful thought; too bad she didn't believe it.

Mr. Moore kept his distance until after the first quarter

when he ambled her way, smiling as though they had known each other for years.

"Good morning. I see you're drinking coffee. Would you like a refill?"

"No, thanks, Mr. Moore, " Anita replied, avoiding his gaze. "I've had enough for the day." *You included.*

"Please call me Regan."

His attempt at friendship bothered her almost as much as his earlier rudeness. She dampened her lips, realizing she owed him the same polite response.

"And call me Anita." She nearly choked on the words. He did have a rugged look about him, if she'd been interested. Besides, if he'd been rude once, he could do it again. And it had better not involve Tyler, or she'd skin the fire marshal and toss him into a boiling pot of her wrath.

Taking a sip of coffee, he smiled through the lashes of his blue-violet eyes. "Do you and Tyler have plans for the rest of the morning?"

"Yes, I've some painting to do." She hoped he felt the same icy chill she so willingly shoved his way.

"Oh, I see."

They spent the next few moments encouraging Tyler's team, then cheering when the boys scored a goal and matched the opponent's score. Watching six year olds scramble for a soccer ball did have its humorous moments. The boys reminded her of flies on honey. The fourth quarter ended in a tie game, which suited her just fine. Tyler took the game too seriously, and when his team lost, he usually blamed himself.

"Thanks for coming, Mr. Moore," Tyler said enthusiastically, flashing his irresistible dark eyes.

"You were great, Tyler. Goalie is a tough position. If the ball gets past the defense, all the heat's on you. Not everyone can take that pressure."

Tyler agreed. "You know about soccer?"

"I used to play in college and coached a little too."

"Wow," the little boy replied, definitely impressed.

Anita felt her heart tighten despite her earlier resolve to be civil. Had Regan majored in impressing little boys too?

"We've got to get going," Anita said to her son, ruffling his hair.

He shrugged. "Okay." He kicked at the grass with the toe of his soccer shoe, not at all like her well-mannered little boy.

"You have a great Saturday," Regan said, bending to Tyler's eye level, "and I'll see you soon."

"I'll be at Grandma's most of the day," Tyler said.

She winced. Now it looked like she pawned off her son while she worked.

Anita feigned a cheery good-bye and climbed into her two-door sensible car, then headed toward her mother's house. Already she envisioned Mom ready to tackle the rest of the morning with Tyler. Theresa Gavanti always planned a surprise of some sort. She'd taken her grandson hiking, bird watching, out to a farm to milk cows, berry picking, and on countless other excursions, most of which ended with a junk-food outing.

Anita admired her mother's energy and enthusiasm for life and believed living near the older woman might be a source of inspiration for rebuilding her own shattered spirit. Mom claimed joy came from the Lord, but Anita felt otherwise. She hadn't been able to separate herself from the scars left after Vince's accident, and she refused to talk to anyone about them.

Suddenly she realized her mother would be asking a mound of questions about the Big Brother project. Well, she certainly didn't plan to sing Regan Moore's praises, but then again, Tyler acted as though the fire marshal stepped off a cloud.

"Oh, my, what did you think of Regan?" Mom asked soon after their arrival.

"He seemed to enjoy Tyler's company," Anita said. "But I'll let him tell you all about it. I need to run, Mom, or I won't get done today. Besides the painting, I need to sort through some new learning centers. Let's talk tonight, okay?"

"Sure, Honey. What about dinner?"

"Sounds wonderful." Pretending to be in a rush, Anita thwarted anymore questions and made her way to the door. She needed time to consider Regan Moore. Painting provided the right atmosphere to sort out her thoughts and come to terms with the fire marshal's association with her son. Truthfully she'd like to find a reason to keep them apart. The only hero Tyler needed was Vince; everyone else ran a bad second.

After placing the new learning centers in the proper rooms and midway through painting the two-year-old room, Anita heard someone pounding on the school door. Thinking it might be one of the ministers or a school board member, she raced down the hall to answer it. Still holding the paintbrush, she stuck the handle in her mouth. Flinging open the door, she saw Regan standing there with a pizza box.

three

"It's lunchtime." Regan grinned and held out the box like a peace offering. "And I thought you might need some nourishment.

She'd felt the pangs of hunger since late morning but had refused to stop working long enough to get something to eat. She really wanted to deliberate more on this man and his interference with her and Tyler's lives—not eat pizza and venture into small talk.

"Are you going to let me in?" he asked. "I promise not to say a word about the paint brush in your mouth, except pizza might taste better."

Anita sensed embarrassment flowing from her head to her toes and removed the paintbrush. "It's very nice of you to bring lunch, but it isn't necessary."

"I wanted to," he said as she ushered him inside. "Besides, it's supposed to be your favorite."

"And what is my favorite?" she asked, suddenly curious.

"A triple cheese with mushrooms and a cheese crust," he said with an air of importance. "Plus a bottle of diet cola to wash it all down."

"How did you know?" She lifted the pizza box from his arms and inhaled the tantalizing aroma. Black coffee hadn't been much of a breakfast.

"A six year old told me. He even told me where to buy it."

"That rascal," Anita said, unable to curb a smile. "It does smell heavenly. Is this all for me, or do I have to share it with you?" Her last remark meant a little more than gratitude. Maybe she should go easier on him.

"I was hoping you'd ask." He pulled the bottle of diet cola

from one pocket and a regular cola from the other.

Since he'd been so thoughtful, she decided to make the most of the situation. "Shall we dine on chairs from a preschool room or a kindergarten room?"

"Don't you have a teacher's lounge?" he asked with a wry smile, then added, "Yes, you do. I remember exactly where it's located."

Anita didn't particularly care for his attempt at charm. Let him amuse Tyler, but she preferred not to join the fire marshal's fan club.

During lunch, he attempted conversation, and she did her best to relax and be amiable. She wished he had displayed some of this pleasantness the previous day.

"Thank you for the pizza." She brushed the crumbs from her lap. "And thanks for watching Tyler's game. He really appreciated it."

He reached for another slice of pizza and took a generous bite. Swallowing, he reached for his drink. "Tyler's a great kid. I'm sure you're proud of him."

"Yes, definitely. He's my whole world."

"I hope you don't mind, especially since we got off to a rough start, but Mrs. Gavanti told me a little about your situation." He wet his lips, and she detected a hint of apprehension in him.

"Oh?" Anita questioned, staring directly into Regan's eyes. She didn't like her personal life leading any topic of conversation. "And what did my mother say?"

He wiped tomato sauce from his mouth with a paper napkin and hesitated. "She said your husband drowned while fishing, and Tyler witnessed the accident."

Anita nodded. Suddenly the food weighed heavy in her stomach. "Yes, and I'm sure she told you all about his nightmares."

"Do you mind explaining to me what happened? I understand if you feel it's none of my business, but if I can establish a relationship with him, maybe I can help."

She deliberated over his request. In one breath, she wanted to tell Regan not to bother with Tyler's problem, and in the other, she knew her son's emotional health was more important than her irritation. None of the counselors had been successful in ridding him of the recurring nightmares, and she doubted if Regan could either, but she refused to discount the remote possibility.

"All right," she said after several long moments. "His counselors urged me to have patience and allow him to work through his emotions, but he's so young, and I hate to see him suffer." Anita swallowed the lump in her throat. "Vince, my husband, and Tyler often went fishing together. It's not my favorite thing to do, and it provided excellent father-son time. Anyway, when Vince fell into the lake, Tyler did exactly what his father had always instructed—stay seated in the boat and if something happens, shout for help. He obeyed. Two hours later, another fishing boat neared the scene, and Tyler offered them a hundred million dollars to find his daddy swimming in the deep water."

"Poor kid." Regan clenched his fist. "How long ago did this happen?"

"Little over two years ago."

"Is he still under the care of a counselor?"

Anita shook her head. "No. Since we moved back to Sweetwell, I haven't had time to interview anyone. I really wondered if moving away from Tulsa might help the nightmares. Truthfully, he has them pretty often."

"Does he relive the accident?"

"Not always. Sometimes he's lost or drowning or someone is making him take swimming lessons. Leaves me feeling helpless."

"I understand how you feel. Love does powerful things when someone is hurting." His voice sounded gentle, almost soothing. Odd, the rigid features so evident yesterday afternoon had vanished. "I haven't much training in Tyler's area, but I promise to do my best."

Anita glanced at him and wondered why he even wanted to help. Granted, she didn't care for the man, and his first impression ruined any thoughts of friendship, but he did represent an excellent organization.

"I will do anything for my son." Anita affirmed her resolution by staring directly into his eyes. "I love him. These nightmares are ruining his childhood, and I'm at my wit's end. If you can shed some light into his life, then you are welcome to do so."

"Were his counselors Christian?" He leaned back in his chair.

Anita hesitated before she answered. After all, she was the director of a Christian School. "No, I wanted only the best for Tyler—you know, more education than a few classes in Bible college. I didn't want the God-thing to interfere with his care."

Regan lifted a brow. "I see. Anita, do you mind if we pray about this?"

She shifted uncomfortably. If she said exactly how she felt about prayer, it might get back to the preschool board. If she consented, she had to sit through Regan's petition to a Deity she'd lost faith in. "Sure," she agreed. "Go right ahead."

Anita listened to Regan pray for healing and guidance in his relationship with Tyler. She tried to listen respectfully, but a mixture of awkwardness and discomfort settled upon her. She'd heard similar prayers before, and nothing had resulted. Why should this one make any difference?

Feeling certain her mother had thoroughly considered Regan's background, Anita decided to talk to her about him after dinner. *Now I wish I hadn't given him permission to pray.*

After he finished, she took a deep breath. "I'm not convinced you can do anything more than what trained professionals have managed. Acting on behalf of the Big Brothers is commendable, but attempting to rid Tyler of an emotional disorder is another. It could cause more harm than good."

She saw a pained expression, similar to what she'd seen yesterday, and she felt a brief twinge of guilt. But Tyler's mental health came first. As his mother and only living parent, she must carefully select his companions and activities. She shouldn't have welcomed Regan to befriend Tyler without doing more research about him.

"I'd really like to try—possibly gain his confidence."

"Why?"

"I like kids, and I want to see them happy and safe—to grow up in God's family with a sense of self-worth."

At last Anita felt she had the upper hand. "I see no harm in social contacts. School starts on Wednesday, and I need to make sure he gets his rest during the week."

Regan nodded. "How does one night a week, then something on the weekends, like a soccer game and breakfast or lunch depending on the game?"

"We can work it out," Anita replied dubiously. She closed the empty pizza box. "Well, I need to get back to work."

He picked up the drink containers and dropped them into the trash. "Can I help?" He jammed his hands into his jeans pockets, a mannerism she'd noticed the previous evening when he seemed nervous.

"It's not necessary. I only have about another hour or so left."

"I came prepared to work."

She smiled, but she'd spent enough of one day with him. She still hadn't taken the time to tuck him into a neat little corner of her mind.

"No, thanks, really. I'd like to finish it myself. I need the solitude to think about school opening." She crossed her arms over her chest. "Thanks again for the pizza. It tasted delicious."

Moments later, Anita watched Regan pull away from the school parking lot. She waved before slowly trudging back down the hallway to the two-year-old room.

Contemplating Regan's outward appearance, she believed

his deep-set eyes and dimpled grin were his most attractive features. He stood about four inches taller than her five foot eight—not too thin or too heavy, sort of average.

Wait a minute, why am I sizing him up like apples at the grocery store? I don't think I even like him. She simply needed to find out more information from her mother. The Big Brother arrangement may not have been such a good idea. And she really wished she hadn't agreed to any of it.

Anita flipped open a can of pale yellow paint and mentally calculated a mid-afternoon completion time. She could then spend the evening with her mother before heading home. Again, she felt relief in knowing her mother lived only moments away instead of miles. The two talked more now than when she lived at home. Possibly their kinship came in the absence of their husbands.

⁊

"Mom, as always you cooked a fantastic dinner." Anita dabbed her mouth with a blue-checked napkin. "You know how I love manicotti. I'll have to run five miles before I can fit through my apartment door."

"Me too, Grandma," Tyler chimed in. "You cook almost as good as Mom."

"Thank you." Her mother clasped her hands together and leaned toward her grandson. "Are you ready for dessert? I made a triple layer chocolate cake."

Even Tyler shook his head and patted his stomach. "I'm too full, but maybe I could take some home for later?" He gave his mother a silent plea.

Anita attempted to give him a stern look, but she laughed instead, knowing her mother had baked the cake especially for him. "Perhaps a little piece wouldn't hurt."

"Or a little extra for tomorrow," Mom said, her round face glowing, "and I'll put in a slice for your mom."

Tyler carried his plate and silverware to the kitchen counter and hurried off outside to play. After a few minutes of chitchat,

Anita's mother eyed her suspiciously. "What's wrong, Honey? It's written all over your face."

Anita offered a faint smile. "That obvious, uh?"

Her mother scooted herself from the table. "Yes, so out with it."

"In two words, Regan Moore."

"Regan? Is he not going to work out for Tyler?" She sounded upset.

Anita took a deep breath. "I'm not sure about it yet. I neglected to tell you he failed the school's fire inspection."

Mom's dark eyes flashed, and she stiffened. "Why? What happened?"

Anita poured them another cup of coffee and added cream and artificial sweetener to her mother's. Taking a deep breath, she told the whole story. "I'm trying to have an open mind about him, and he did apologize. But how can I trust him with Tyler knowing he can be rather nasty? Plus, he wants an opportunity to help with the nightmares."

"Regan would never do anything to harm a child," her mother said, sadness spreading across her face.

Anita viewed the tiny lines around her mother's eyes. Dark strands wove through silver hair, softening the telltale signs of age. "Maybe you should tell me about the man, because I'm confused and frustrated. I know you respect him, or you wouldn't have recommended him."

Her mother nodded. "I agree he could have been more understanding about the paint cans, but there's a reason behind his behavior. You see, nearly four years ago, about this time of year. . ." She stood abruptly from the table and headed for the kitchen, leaving Anita short of bewildered. A moment later, she returned with a calendar. "This makes sense."

"Mom, I don't know what you're talking about."

She set the calendar aside and pulled her chair to the table. "Regan's wife and little daughter were killed in a tragic house fire four years ago. I believe yesterday was the anniversary of their deaths, and you said his grandmother died. I remember the date because the church had a huge grounds clean-up on that day. Anyway, he'd just been appointed fire marshal and was at the station house when the call came through. He rode with the crew to extinguish the blaze."

"How terrible." Anita shuddered, rubbing an eerie chill from her arms.

"It gets worse. Regan found his wife and daughter in their bedroom where the two had been napping together. They'd been overcome with smoke. For a long time, he struggled with their deaths and blamed himself."

Anita blinked back the tears, reliving a fraction of her own pain in losing Vince. She couldn't have lived another moment if Tyler had been taken from her too. "Now I understand his obsession with the rules regarding fire safety. I wonder how he can work in his position with those horrible memories. I mean, Mom, it must be a constant reminder of their deaths."

"I'm not sure how he does it, but I know his faith is firmly rooted in Jesus Christ. Honey, he really is a good man. I'm sure losing his grandmother along with facing the anniversary of his family's tragic deaths triggered his abrupt behavior. Please believe me, I thought he'd do a magnificent job with Tyler. He dearly loves kids, and he volunteers a great deal of his time to the church youth."

"Well, Tyler adores him," Anita replied. "I wish I'd known his background. Then I could have been more understanding."

Her mother reached across the table and patted her daughter's hand. "I'm sure he's had his share of nightmares. You know, Regan may be able to work wonders with our Tyler."

"You're wanting me to try, aren't you?" Anita nibbled on her lip. She remembered how jealous she'd been of Regan last night and today with Tyler. *I thought I was above that type of thing, but I guess not.*

"Nothing else has worked, and I've prayed for a miracle."

Anita took another sip of coffee. "All right. I'll talk to Regan this week."

The gravity of the man's situation shook her again. She couldn't imagine facing the horror of losing a child and a spouse. The devastation of Vince's death had pushed her into severe depression, and her regular physician had prescribed antidepressants for more than a year until she'd flushed them down the toilet when they didn't help. After two years, she still sank into dark pits of despair. Blame and guilt stalked her like a haunting shadow. If she'd been a better wife: encouraged more, been more loving, cooked better, kept a cleaner house, exercised more, given him another child, accompanied him and Tyler when they went fishing. The list of ways she might have prevented Vince from drowning proved endless.

Regan must possess inner strength, but she didn't know how she felt about his attributing his healing to God. How long had it been since her spiritual life meant more than it did now? She'd closed the door on God when Vince died. In short, God's sense of fairness didn't appeal to her, and He'd continued to make life difficult. No, she didn't need God to tangle up her mind. She'd had enough of life's complications.

four

Monday morning at Good Hope Christian Preschool sped by with the phone ringing non-stop. Most of the calls were parents making last-minute requests to register their children for the fall session. Teachers and aides bustled about their rooms—exchanging ideas, adding final touches to room decorations, and making sure their supplies were ready for the first day of little students.

The building hummed with activity, and somewhere Anita heard a recording of children's voices blended in song. Her teachers were a great group and worked well together. The school year looked promising, filled with exciting programs and activities.

Before lunch, the sweet, rich smell of oatmeal raisin cookies wafted through the building. The cook had decided to treat them all with one of her specialties. The only thing remaining for school to open was the fire inspection report and a signed license from the Department of Human Services.

Shortly before noon, Anita found herself alone. She loved the business of the morning, but she required solitude to finish her own pile of work. A stack of papers slowly dwindled from her desktop as she processed each child's application and entered the information into her computer.

The bell above the front door jingled lightly, announcing a visitor. Anita glanced up to see Regan dressed in his uniform, but this time he didn't sport a frown.

"Good afternoon, Anita," he greeted her pleasantly.

A warm gaze met hers, and for an instant, she felt herself grow uncomfortable. "Hi. Is it noon already?"

"Sure is. I have a signed inspection report for you." He

retrieved a piece of paper from beneath his clipboard.

"Don't you want to see the school first?" she asked, more than slightly surprised with his change of attitude.

"I suppose I should. But after the ordeal I put you through last Friday, I figure there's not a paint can within miles." He smiled, and Anita easily returned the gesture. The incident seemed forgotten in light of what she'd learned about him. In its place rested sympathy. . .and empathy.

"I wouldn't want you going against protocol," she replied. "Besides, I'd like for you to see my staff getting ready for the first day of school." Rising from her desk, she escorted him through every room and introduced him to each person they met.

Upon completion, Anita gratefully took the signed fire inspection. "Thank you. I appreciate your coming before my one o'clock appointment."

"My pleasure." A smile lingered on his lips. In fact, he hadn't stopped smiling.

They stood side by side while awkward moments ticked by. Anita wished he'd leave, but she could tell he intended to say more. Still, she should make some comment regarding Tyler.

"Tyler wanted me to tell you hello," she finally said.

His gaze caught hers, and the steely blue pools she stared into reflected compassion. "Do you have anything planned for him tomorrow night?"

Anita hesitated and remembered her commitment to her mother and Tyler. "Hmm, he does have soccer practice from five to six-thirty."

"Can I pick him up and take him to eat afterwards?"

She swallowed a hint of jealousy, knowing she didn't want to share her son with anyone. She could refuse; mothers had the right, but. . . "I suppose that's okay. It's at the same field where he played on Saturday."

A funny little flutter in the bottom of her stomach caused

her to shift her attention to the inspection report. *What is wrong with me?*

"Thanks, and I'll have him home early."

Anita walked him to the door. "Regan, could we talk afterwards? I mean, would you have time to stick around until I put him to bed?"

A startled look swept over his rugged features. "Sure."

She felt herself grow increasingly warm. The air conditioner's thermostat must be up too high. "To discuss Tyler and firm up definite times to see him." *Great, now I sound like a single mom working out visitations with an ex-husband.*

"Sounds like an excellent idea."

"Good. Tyler will be so excited to spend some time with you."

He grasped the doorknob, then swung his gaze back her way. "You're welcome to come along."

The look Regan gave Anita sent chills to her toes and burned her face at the same time. The words to the children's song "Oh Susanna" flashed across her mind. *The sun so hot, I froze to death. . .*

She wet her lips and tried desperately to remember his question. While humiliation oozed from the pores of her skin, she focused on the pale green wallpaper swirled in a marble effect.

"We could swing by and pick you up after soccer practice."

As though pinched, she remembered. "No, thanks, but I'm grateful for the offer."

"Another time then?"

For a moment, she lost herself in the smile teasing at his lips. "Oh, sure. It. . .it probably is a good time to establish your relationship with Tyler."

"I'm hoping to. See you tomorrow."

Anita hoped he couldn't tell she struggled with every word. "Sure. Have a good day."

Once the metal door closed, she leaned back against it for support and closed her eyes. Her disturbing reaction to Regan left her bewildered and a little angry. She didn't even like the man. If her mother hadn't been so insistent about his wonderful involvement in the Big Brothers program, Anita wouldn't have given him a second glance. But Tyler needed a good male companion.

She must simply be stressed with school opening. Yes, the weight of opening the new school must be the answer.

"He is good looking."

Anita instantly opened her eyes to find one of her teachers, Susan Walters, observing her with a wide grin.

"I hadn't noticed," Anita said, crossing her arms and heading to her desk.

"Right." Susan laughed, her eyes sparkling. "We went to high school together, remember? This reminds me of the time when you got caught passing notes in government class."

"What does that have to do with now?"

"You had the same guilty look on your face."

❧

Regan gripped the steering wheel of his Jeep, his knuckles white and his mind spinning in a vortex of confusion. What happened back there? One minute he'd invited Anita to join him and Tyler for supper, and the next, he'd found himself imprisoned by a pair of blue and amber shackles—complete with extra long lashes.

He hadn't noticed her eyes before, pale blue with streaks of gold. Oh, he'd seen the lightning flash when he'd made her angry, and he'd deserved it. But today, well, guess he'd been taken by surprise.

Regan sighed and turned down Evergreen Street en route to Sweetwell's Fellowship Church for his grandmother's funeral. He sure regretted Anita seeing the nasty side of him last Friday. Between the news about his grandmother and the anniversary of his wife and daughter's deaths, he'd been in a foul mood. Four years ago, and sometimes the memories were as vivid as yesterday. He could still see the blinding smoke, hear the crackling fire, feel the burning in his throat, and hear his own voice screaming for Carey and little Brenna. The nightmare inside the bedroom had haunted him until Jesus took away the pain. And sometimes, like last Friday, he had to turn off the old tapes playing inside his head and toss them in the trash. He simply had to cling to his Lord.

More than anything, he wanted Tyler to know the same peace.

"Thank You, Lord, for bringing me through those days," he whispered. Now, when he started to sink, God threw out the lifeline and reeled him in. Tyler needed God's help—no child should be tormented with such bad dreams.

Or his mother, either. Regan could only imagine the emotional anguish Anita must go through each time Tyler had a nightmare.

He recalled Theresa Gavanti describing her daughter as a solid Christian, but he'd heard Anita's apathy toward God. Little things she said and the look of indifference on her face when he suggested prayer indicated a problem with her faith. Bitterness perhaps. He well remembered blaming God for taking Carey and Brenna from him. It took him a long time before he realized his family now lived in heaven. Yes, he missed them, but they were in a perfect place. His life held purpose and meaning, and with that knowledge he lived each day for the Lord.

He drove down a residential area with stately two- and three-story homes. Most had been restored to their original beauty, grand red bricks, glimmering white painted homes with huge porches and hanging ferns, and gingerbread Victorians painted in pastel colors. In the middle of all the lovely homes stood a dilapidated structure in which workmen had just begun renovation. Shingles hung lopsided, pieces of roofing lay scattered about on the ground, and the front door rested on its hinges. Even with the windows up on his Jeep, he could hear the sawing and hammering.

He'd looked much like that shabby dwelling before God went to work rebuilding him from the inside out.

Regan smiled. *Getting philosophical in my old age. The back side of thirty must do strange things to a person.*

He pulled into the parking lot of Fellowship Church. He hadn't been to a funeral since the day he'd buried his family. This was hard. Although he knew funerals were a celebration of life, it brought back bad memories. For certain, his grandmother no longer suffered with brain cancer. She'd been healed.

Once parked, he leaned against the steering wheel and stared up at the blue sky growing darker and menacing in the distance—much like the inner turmoil of the past few days. He cringed with his own reflections. If he analyzed everything like this at age thirty-six, imagine what he'd be like at forty-six. Probably ready to write a self-help book.

Regan turned off the engine. A score of friends emerged from their vehicles, while others moved slowly toward the entrance. Most of them were older people, men shuffling along in dark suits and women carrying their purses as if they were walking canes.

He stepped from his Jeep at the same time Mrs. Gavanti pulled up in her apple red sports car. She waved, and he waited for her. A moment later, she grasped both sides of the door and climbed out.

"Good afternoon, Regan," Mrs. Gavanti said with a smile, being careful to lock her door. "I'm so sorry to hear about your grandmother."

"Thank you, and I appreciate your coming." He saw she wore a bright orange and green print dress with a black scarf. Colorful, just like the lady before him.

"Why, your grandmother and my mother were best friends. I loved her like family."

Regan smiled. "Yeah, she was a pretty special lady."

Mrs. Gavanti gripped the would-be waist of her dress and

gave it a twist. "My slip hanging?"

He muffled a laugh, disguising it as a cough, and took a few steps behind her. "Hmm, just a little on the left side."

She grimaced and gave the waist a tug again. "Oh, fishhooks, guess I'll have to visit the powder room."

"It's not that bad," he said, keeping stride with her again. "Barely noticeable, in fact."

"Humph," she replied. "I bet. Nothing I can do about it now. Say, how did it go with Tyler last weekend?"

"Very good, but I'm sure you heard all about it, especially my blunder on Friday. I'm sure you got an earful.

She patted his arm. "I saw the date on the calendar, and Della's passing had to make it a rough day."

"Didn't make it right, though. Does Anita know. . ."

"Yes. I told her."

"Guess that's best. I apologized, but I'll have to be next-to-perfect to redeem myself. At least she's allowing me to see Tyler. You were right; he's a great kid."

"Of course," she said with a knowing nod.

He noticed the amber streaks in her blue eyes. As many times as he'd visited with Mrs. Gavanti, he'd not paid attention to the unique color.

"Is something wrong?" the older woman asked, leaning closer.

Regan shook his head, feeling a bit awkward with his scrutiny. "No, not at all. I'm fine."

She smiled. "I'm glad you'll be working with my grandson. Like I warned you before, my daughter is hurting in a big way. I know I told you, but she used to be closer to the Lord. Sometimes I think she wouldn't be going to church at all if I didn't insist. She's not involved in a Sunday school class, and I pick Tyler up early for his little group. I'm sorry for not being open about that earlier."

"I understand." He opened the intricately carved church door and ushered Mrs. Gavanti inside.

"Well, I think you are the perfect medicine for Tyler—and Anita." With those words, she teetered down the hallway to the ladies' room.

Regan shook his head at the loveable, unpredictable Theresa Gavanti. Certainly nothing like her daughter—except the eyes. Anita Todd, with her proper mannerisms and tall, slender frame. She did have the same coffee-colored, wavy, rich-looking hair, but she wore a melancholy smile, as though she felt destined to spend the rest of her life devoid of happiness.

He remembered feeling the same anguish.

He glanced about and saw his parents talking to another couple near the entrance of the sanctuary. Their gazes met, and he moved across the foyer to meet them.

"You doing all right, Dad?" Regan placed a comforting hand on his father's shoulder.

"Yes, I'm okay—just want to put Mother to rest," the balding man replied.

"Looks like half the town is here for the service."

The elder Moore seemed to take note of the crowd. "I believe you're right. Your mom was reminding me you hadn't been to a funeral in four years. This is a hard day for you too."

Regan crammed his hands inside his suit pants pockets. "Right."

His dad sighed. "So now I ask, are you all right?"

"Yeah. Of course the day brings back painful memories and there's the grief from losing Grandmother, but I know God is with us through all of this."

Regan reached over to give his mother a quick kiss on the cheek and take her hand. This dear woman who shared his light coloring had been a pillar of strength on more than one occasion. "Let's go inside and get seated," she said. "I hear the music, and it's one of your grandmother's favorite hymns."

Amidst the soft sounds of the organ playing "I'll Fly Away," the three took their places in a front pew. Regan suddenly felt at ease, peaceful. Count on God to bring His blessings when he needed them most.

The air smelled sweetly of roses, ushering in unwanted memories. He shook his head and noted the host of flower arrangements and green potted plants placed around the casket. Grandmother had touched the lives of so many people. Hopefully, he could do the same.

A picture of Anita and her son Tyler flashed across his mind. If only he could change the rotten start with the boy's mother. First impressions had a habit of sticking.

The afternoon proved to last a little longer than Regan would have liked, and by the time the graveside services and the dinner back at the church fellowship hall were over, he simply wanted to get home. He'd stayed until the last guest left, urging his parents to head home, then he'd helped clean up the hall. When he finally walked to the parking lot for his own trek home, weariness overtook him, and he imagined Anita often felt the same way with the weight of a job and single parenting.

God had brought her to Sweetwell for a reason, and he prayed she and Tyler would find the healing they so desperately needed.

five

For what seemed like the hundredth time, Anita took another glimpse at her watch. Regan and Tyler were precisely five minutes late. Against her better judgment, she had consented for Regan to take her son back and forth to soccer practice, then to dinner. By all of her calculations, eating should have taken all of thirty minutes at any fast-food restaurant, allow ten, max fifteen minutes to drive home, and five more to park Regan's Jeep and climb the stairs to the second-story apartment. Even if she considered hitting all of the lights red, they should have been there. Presto, now they were six minutes late.

Regan could have at least called and informed me of their whereabouts. That would have been the considerate gesture. Maybe I should try to find them—call his cell phone. After all, there are only four fast-food spots in town—hamburger, pizza, chicken, and an ice cream and fast-food combo.

Irritation spiked its way to the tilt level. Again she stared at her watch and decided when they were fifteen minutes late, she'd phone him. She should have set down guidelines before they'd left. This anxiety was her fault.

At exactly fourteen and three-quarters to Anita's allotted time, she heard a knock at the door. She jumped like a startled feline and hurried to the door, certain the headlines in tomorrow's paper would read "Local Woman Succumbs to a Pounding Heart."

"Hi, Mom." Tyler reached up to give her a hug.

She trembled slightly, certain her tears were ready to assault her cheeks, and allowed him to give her one of his vise-grip holds. "I expected you sooner."

43

"I'm sorry." Regan leaned against the door jam. "We ate at Uncle Billy's."

That explains it, a real restaurant.

"Hmm." Tyler rubbed his stomach. "I ate a whole chicken fried steak with mashed 'tatoes and gravy—and vegetables."

Regan chuckled. "We splurged since he'd had a good practice. Didn't let a single goal get passed him, did you, Sport?" He ruffled Tyler's hair, sending pea-green sensations to Anita's heart.

"I assumed you'd head for hamburgers and fries." She broke from Tyler's strangling hold and studied her son's face; his mouth and lips looked like he'd sucked on a piece of coal. "Whatever did you eat that was black?" For a moment, she wondered if the two had indulged in Uncle Billy's blackberry cobbler.

She lifted a questioning brow to Regan whose lips were also stained.

"Licorice." Tyler displayed his missing teeth and a wide, black smile. "Mr. Regan keeps it in his Jeep."

Anita shuddered. "Tyler, licorice is the nastiest candy ever made."

"No, it's really good, Mom. Here, bend down a minute."

She allowed Regan to step inside the apartment, then bent for Tyler to plant a kiss on her cheek. Tyler giggled. "Now you have the mark of the black lips."

A vision of her son's dark imprint on her cheek made her laugh. "And what's the mark supposed to mean?"

"Only the one who loves you can give it to you." Tyler beamed and stole a look at Regan.

How sweet. "Then I qualify, don't I?" Anita hugged him.

"Right. You're the best mom in the whole world, better than those silly old girls at school."

Before she had time to expound on the good qualities of little girls, Tyler added, "Mr. Regan, why don't you give Mom a kiss and see if it shows up black on her face?"

For yet another embarrassing moment, of which she'd had her share since meeting Regan, Anita didn't know whether to apologize or say nothing. And she refused to catch his gaze.

"I think I'll pass this time," Regan said hastily.

Thank you, Mr. Moore.

"Why?" Tyler stared up at the fire marshal.

Regan cleared his throat. "I don't think it works on the same person twice."

"Oh, okay." Tyler nodded thoughtfully. "Tell you what. Next time I'll let you kiss Mom, so it's fair."

Reaching the bottom of the humiliation scale, Anita quickly captured the moment. "Tyler, did you thank Mr. Regan for everything he did for you tonight?"

"Yes, Ma'am, in the Jeep."

"Good. Why don't you get your bath while he and I visit?" *If we can recover from the licorice kisses comments.* "From the looks of your clothes, the field must have been muddy. I'll fill the tub while you get your pajamas." She turned to Regan, determined for him to see her calm and poised. "I'll be with you in just a moment. Make yourself at home." She gestured toward the living room. "Iced tea is in the fridge."

Although Tyler offered a faint groan, he did set his sights on the bathroom. She ran the tub with a mountain of bubbles and reminded him of the dirt behind his ears. His hair needed to be washed, but they'd have time in the morning.

While Tyler played with a menagerie of tub animals, which he'd never own up to, Anita took a seat at the opposite end of the couch from Regan. She groped for something to say. "We have a few moments before he's finished. Would you like more iced tea?"

He laid aside a magazine for parents. She glanced to see what he'd been reading—an article on communicating with your child. "No, thank you." He rubbed his palms together. "Anita, I'm sorry about the licorice—"

"It's all right," she interrupted. *Let's not go there again.*

Once is enough. "Tyler tends to be rather spontaneous."

"I noticed."

"But licorice? I guess I should have been glad it wasn't sugary blue bubblegum." Suddenly the whole episode exploded into hilarity. "You should have seen your face." Anita covered her mouth. "Reminded me of a rock group—the ones who paint their faces white and wear black lipstick." The teasing relaxed her a bit, but she still felt immensely uncomfortable.

"Me? I'd say yours was a healthy shade of red—about the color of my Jeep." Regan studied her for a long moment, as though contemplating what to say.

She smelled his aftershave, dangerously intoxicating, but she didn't feel any attraction to him. Not in the least.

"We sure are having a rough start at friendship, and so far I have to take the blame." He looked about as awkward as she felt.

"Oh, I haven't been exactly cooperative." She slowly allowed her tense body to ease against the sofa. "And I might as well admit I'm very possessive of my son."

"Under the circumstances, who can blame you?" All traces of teasing vanished. Concern lines plowed across his brow.

Maybe you aren't such a bad guy after all. "He's all I have, Regan, and I want him to have a normal childhood."

"I understand. You want what every good parent desires for their child."

She took a deep breath and grasped the courage to stare into the depth of his eyes. "I think you do too. That's why I'm giving you the opportunity to help with his nightmares. I know I agreed to this before, but my heart wasn't totally sold on the idea—"

"Until your mother told you what happened to my family?"

Finish what you started, Girl. She nodded. "I have to push my protective nature aside and seek Tyler's best interests. Guess I needed to state that more for myself than you."

He offered a slight smile. "I can't help him alone, but only through God." The God-thing rankled at her nerves, but before she could comment, Regan continued. "I know this will be tough. You and I have to pool our efforts and work together. Communication is the key. Every little thing we notice out of the ordinary with Tyler should be relayed to the other. You may be the one to break the pattern by finding out something you didn't know before."

Do you have any idea how difficult this will be for me? But I don't really have a choice. She hesitated. "I agree."

"Anita?"

She whirled her attention back to him.

"Can you handle spending time with me as we work with Tyler through this?" His voice sounded low with a note of strength against the backdrop of her frayed emotions. "People will talk and assume a relationship between us, but I don't see any other way to handle it."

"For Tyler, I'd do anything." She hoped he heard and saw her resolve.

꙳

Anita desperately needed for her nerves to settle, but the line of cars waiting to drop off children for the first day of school on Wednesday left her somewhere between alarmed and thrilled. The morning sky, polished as bright as a child's beaming face, offered promise and hope. The staff acted equally as excited. She took a deep breath mixed with the freshness of small town living and a sultry wind carrying the scent of roses from a nearby home.

Anita tingled to the bottom of her toes. Like a child anticipating Christmas, she couldn't sleep the night before. For weeks she'd envisioned the children filling the rooms with their little bodies and hearing their sweet laughter. The opportunity to fill a child's mind with hope and a desire for learning had always been her goal. She wanted to make an impact on these children's lives, one that prepared them for elementary school through college with a positive experience.

As she stood inside looking through the front window, waiting for the time to greet the first vehicle in the circular driveway, she recalled her commitment to early childhood education so many years ago. Those were college days over-flowing with all the ideals of changing the world.

A trace of bittersweet nipped at her heart. Vince. . .just when she least expected it, he crept into her thoughts. They'd met at a Campus Crusade for Christ meeting; seemed like a lifetime ago. Lately she'd found it harder to remember what he looked like without looking at his picture on her night-stand. The best she could do was watch Tyler and see the traits of his father, the man he'd someday be.

I will not spoil today. Vince knew my heart for children. Her life now centered on her son, his emotional healing, and her position at Good Hope School. With renewed determina-tion, she pushed the past along with its heartache to a far cor-ner of her mind.

"Do you plan to do this all by yourself?" Susan Walters asked from behind her.

Anita whirled around to her friend, a strawberry blond who hadn't changed her spunky attitude since they'd walked the halls of Sweetwell High. "You know, I forgot all about calling for your help. Don't know what I was thinking, because I can't unload all of these vehicles alone."

"Is your mind on the good-looking fire marshal?" Susan's eyes widened, as though she already knew the answer.

Anita gave her a sideways glance. "Are you serious? He's just a friend."

"Famous last words. I saw the way you gawked at him, remember? You had that what-a-hunk look in your eyes."

"Oh, no, I didn't, and you aren't any more reformed than you were in high school."

Susan's tanned face glowed. "I take that as a compliment, since I'm two kids and ten pounds heavier."

"Aside from your teasing, we are going to have fun, aren't

we? Almost as good as being cheerleaders again."

"I wouldn't miss working with you and these children for the world. I'm so looking forward to my class, and I know they will be little angels. At least they were during home visits."

Anita laughed. "Wonderful. We'll see if their good behavior lasts after the first week."

Susan narrowed her gaze. "Did you put all the little rotten ones in my four-year-old group?"

Anita giggled. How long had it been since she'd shared fun moments with her dear friend? "Would I do such a horrible thing?"

"You bet. I remember the pranks you pulled in high school."

Appearing indignant, Anita whispered just in case any of the other staff were listening. "Like what? Name one."

"Hiding the other cheerleaders' towels during PE. Replacing the dead frogs in biology destined for dissection for live ones. How about the—"

"That's enough. I remember."

"Good. Now you see why I think you'll be the biggest problem kid at school."

Anita stole another look at her watch. The time had come to greet the new students. Stepping into the morning sunshine, she smiled and waved at a minivan parked at the head of the line filled with children. Melodious laughter echoed from the vehicle. Jack-in-the-box bodies bounced up and down shouting, "Here she comes."

She opened the minivan door to their delighted squeals. "Good morning. I'm so excited about your first day of school."

Moving back to Sweetwell had been an excellent idea. She welcomed the opportunity to start her life all over and put some sense into her miserable state. But more importantly, Tyler had a chance to fill his childhood with sweet new memories. And maybe Regan Moore might accomplish what she deemed impossible.

six

The day rolled by as near to perfect as Anita could imagine. As expected, a few tears had fallen during the day from those who weren't quite ready for the separation—and some of those tears were from the mothers. One dad sobbed in his car for nearly fifteen minutes after his son told him good-bye. Cameras and camcorders were attached to the parents like extra appendages. The phone still rang nonstop with parents seeking spots for their children or checking on ones left in her care.

For the first time since her arrival three months ago, Anita sensed a new home, a place where she belonged. In Sweetwell, she'd been met with loving arms and a deep sense of sympathy because of Vince's death; however, at Good Hope School she was an equal and appreciated for what she knew and represented.

All of the children were scheduled to stay until two-thirty. The four year olds took a nap from twelve-thirty to two, but the kindergarten classes rested for thirty minutes, then continued with their schoolwork for the remainder of the session. Soon the first day would come to an end. Some of the parents planned to pick up their children at the circular driveway, and others optioned to park their cars so they could visit with their child's teacher. Anita had initiated certain security measures for either choice.

At two o'clock, a man entered the school and pleasantly greeted her at the desk.

"Good afternoon, Mrs. . . ."

"Todd."

"Are you the director?" When she replied affirmatively, he

continued, "I'm Craig Harringer. I apologize for arriving early, but I'm anxious to see my daughter after her first day of school."

She smiled. "I understand, Sir."

"May I take her now?"

"Is she preschool or kindergarten?"

"Preschool."

Anita nodded and offered a smile. "Well, that's an extra point for your case. If she attended kindergarten, I'd have to stick to the two-thirty time frame."

"I appreciate your help." Mr. Harringer looked about. "This is a good looking building."

"Thank you. We're all very proud of our school." She opened her file drawer. "Now, what is your daughter's name?"

"Leesa Harringer."

"Just a moment while I pull her records. Do you remember your password or her teacher's name?"

"No, Ma'am. Sorry, I forgot to get the information." Mr. Harringer, a rather good-looking, muscular man, oozed with charm.

"I'll need your driver's license." Anita lifted the file from the drawer.

While he opened his wallet, she read down through Leesa's release form. Instantly, an alarm sounded in her mind. Craig Harringer and his wife were divorced, and the father didn't have any visitation rights. A copy of the court order denying Craig access to his daughter had been attached to the child's application.

"I'm sorry, Mr. Harringer." Anita peered up and met his gaze. His earlier charm now infuriated her. "I have a legal document here stating you cannot pick up Leesa."

He leaned across the counter, his now-hardened features mere inches from her face. "You will give me my daughter."

She scooted back her chair. "I will not." The words sounded weak to her ears, but unmistakably resolute.

He reached for the file in her hand, but she clamped her fingers around it.

"No one keeps me from Leesa. Do you understand?" he asked through clenched lips. "I am her father, and I have my rights."

"Then discuss it with your attorney, Mr. Harringer. I am bound by law to abide by this court order." She battled fear of the man before her with a boldness she'd not known existed.

He whirled around and unleashed a feral shout as though incensed beyond human logic. Before Anita could gather any composure, his hands swept across the top of an antique buffet, sending parent handouts sailing around the room. An English ivy in a teddy bear pot splattered on the floor.

"You think you have a school? I'll show you I mean business." As if his detonation had not satisfied his rage, he pulled the buffet from the wall and sent it crashing to the floor.

The children. He might hurt the children or one of the staff. Trembling, Anita snatched up the phone and shakily punched in 911. "Hurry, please, send the police." Her voice quivered. "Good Hope Christian Day School. I'm afraid for the children."

"Put that phone down!"

Her heart tightened, hammering until she thought it might burst from her chest. "I've called the police. They're on their way. You're about to get caught."

"I'm not afraid of any of your threats." He turned his attention to the hallway away from her view. The rooms were merely seconds from his fiery temper.

For the first time she regretted her open door policy, originally designed to protect the teacher and the children from any malicious accusations. Unless the teachers had heard the disruption and taken the initiative to shut their doors, the children were listening to this mad man shout obscenities. Sweet, innocent babes who were to be sheltered and protected at all cost.

Instantly Anita arose to face Mr. Harringer. Courage beyond her understanding propelled her to the entrance of the hallway.

"You don't want to try and stop me," he said in a low voice.

But I must! You won't take Leesa or hurt anyone. "I will do whatever is necessary for the welfare of these children."

A siren's shrill call split the air. Mr. Harringer whipped his focus to the front door. Eyes narrowed, he shot a silent dagger before tearing through the front door.

Anita nearly collapsed in the wake of his leaving. She sucked in air and grabbed the wall, nearly tripping over the splintered buffet. *I can't fall apart. I must check on the classes.*

She set her sights on the hallway. The doors were all closed—probably with a teacher and an aide on the opposite side leaning against it. *Thank You, God, if You're really there.* Moistening her lips, Anita arched her back and headed to the first door.

"It's Anita, Mrs. Carlson," she said after a quick knock. Her voice sounded much more confident than she truly felt, and she wondered where the strength came from. "Everything is okay. You can prepare the children for their parents."

Slowly, the door opened, and Anita offered a timid smile to the older woman who taught one of the kindergarten classes. "Is he. . .gone?"

"Yes," Anita whispered. "The police are due here any second. Please keep the children calm as we dismiss them."

The sound of the bell on the front door alerted Anita to two policemen.

"Mrs. Carlson, would you send your aide to inform the other classes that they should proceed with dismissal in a calm fashion?" She successfully hid her trembling with a mask of professionalism. *My position, my responsibilities come first.*

The woman nodded, and Anita ventured toward the police. Her head pounded, and exhaustion crippled her mind. What had happened to the perfect first day of school?

&

At first when Regan heard the sirens, he paid scant attention, but when he heard multiples, he checked on the call. The 911 call to Good Hope Christian Day School sent a chill up his spine. He rushed from his office, leaving a drawer open and an E-mail half answered.

Anita would not phone for emergency help unless she had a crisis.

Slamming his Jeep into reverse, Regan left the parking lot in a manner more befitting a reckless teenager. At that moment, he didn't care. What concerned him lay in a frenzied combination of anxiety for Anita and all the children and teachers at the preschool. She hadn't called for an ambulance but police—something about a problem with a man.

In record time, Regan made it to the school just as parents arrived to pick up their kids. A sharp glance to the entrance showed two police cars with their lights flashing. Regan whipped his vehicle into the church's parking lot and set out on foot toward the school. He wanted to run, but his fast pace would only distress the parents.

"Aren't you a member of the fire department?" a woman asked, attempting to calm a crying baby in the back seat.

Regan offered her a smile, anticipating her next question. "Yes, I am."

"Do you know what's going on inside the school? Is there a fire threat too?" Obviously she recognized his uniform.

He moved toward the open window of her car. "No, Ma'am, but I'm sure the school's staff and the police have the situation under control."

"Then why are you here?"

Good question. "Curious, and I know the director and a few of the teachers." He pointed to the gray-bricked building. "This is my church."

"I see." The woman eyed him suspiciously. "First day of

school and already the police are involved. Makes we wonder if I want my child to continue attending."

"I can certainly understand your concern." Regan glanced at the school and saw Susan Walters and Beth Carlson escorting children to their parents. "It does have an excellent reputation. I know the teachers are accredited with national standards." *Please, Lady. I want to see for myself.* "Everything must be fine because the children are being escorted to the cars."

The woman didn't reply so Regan seized the opportunity to head to the school. He'd feel so much better if Anita stood outside the building with those women. Surely she hadn't been hurt.

"Anita's inside," Susan said quietly as she ushered two little boys to an SUV.

Regan nodded and stepped inside the school. Papers were strewn everywhere, and the antique buffet he'd seen on previous visits now lay in pieces. No child did this. Two policemen—one, Jordan Haller, of whom he knew from Big Brothers—stood with Anita by her desk. Their large frames concealed her face. *Who did this?*

"Thank you, Mrs. Todd," Jordan said. "We've had problems with Mr. Harringer before. You're smart to press charges. Would you like for us to give you a hand with this mess?" He took a step toward the broken furniture and scattered papers.

Anita appeared disoriented. Her chest rose and fell as she stared at the shattered remains of the furniture piece. "Uh, no. I'll get it."

"Jordan, I'll help with this," Regan offered.

The policeman turned. "Hey, Regan. Thanks. Mrs. Todd is pretty shook up. She had a bad experience this afternoon." He gave Anita a business card. "Don't hesitate to call. We'll be in touch."

"The problem's handled?" Regan asked, wanting desperately to know why the front office lay in shambles.

"It soon will be," his friend replied. "This character never goes far."

Once they left, Regan studied Anita. She looked ghastly pale and shook like an autumn leaf. "Why don't you sit down until you get your bearings? Are you really okay?"

She took in a deep breath before replying. "I think I'm fine." Her gaze wandered around the room. As if programmed to dive into the next crisis, she knelt on the floor and began gathering up the papers.

He joined her, stepping aside to let Susan and a couple pint-sized girls exit the school.

"Looks like something broke," one freckle-faced little girl said, peering down at Anita. "Do you want some help?"

"No, thank you, Sweetheart." She gave the child a smile, but he saw how her fingers trembled.

Regan continued to pick up papers, hoping he was assisting her and not making matters worse. "When we're finished, will you tell me what happened? I'd like to help."

She nodded and quickly diverted her attention. Too late, he saw the tears brimming in her eyes. "I don't ever want to face Craig Harringer again, at least not without a policeman."

This has to be Jacob Harringer's son. As badly as he wanted answers, Regan knew Anita had responsibilities until all the children had left for the day. Over the next few minutes, she faced a bombardment of several parents demanding answers to the afternoon's uncanny event.

"I'll have a letter in the morning explaining why the police were summoned," she reassured one distraught parent. She displayed more grace than he would have mustered given the same circumstances.

"Well, my child won't be back. This has really upset me. Imagine having to call the police on the first day of school," the woman said.

"If you will postpone your decision to withdraw your child until after you read the letter, I'm sure it will assure you of your child's safety at all times." No trace of emotion creased Anita's face, but her pallor gave away the inner turmoil. "I'm sure you will then appreciate my position this afternoon."

In the middle of her explanation, Pastor Miller phoned. He'd been detained at the hospital but had heard the news. "Yes, I'm fine; I assure you." Anita stole a look at Regan. "I'm not alone. Besides the staff, Regan Moore is here with me." She inhaled sharply. "Yes, I plan to compose one this evening. I'll phone you with the contents when it's completed." She paused. "No, Pastor Miller, it's not necessary to stop by, but I thank you for your concern."

By this time Susan, whose face reflected the stress of whatever had transpired earlier that afternoon, stood beside Anita. "The police will pick him up, you can depend on it." She wrapped her arm around Anita's shoulders.

Regan couldn't stand it any longer. "What happened?" He'd begun to feel like a broken record.

Anita swallowed hard and described how Craig Harringer had tried to pick up his daughter and his resulting violence when Anita had refused.

"You were incredible," Susan said. "You didn't back down for one minute."

"It wasn't me saying those things." Anita moved from the shelter of Susan's arm to reclaim the rest of the papers on the floor.

"Right, it was God protecting you and the rest us from harm's way."

"Possibly, and thanks," Anita whispered, apparently concentrating on the floor.

Regan's heart lifted with hope. This might be a step in the right direction. *Oh, Lord, Anita needs to see Your hand in this today. Thanks for protecting her and all the others here.*

"I simply thought of each child as my own, as if Tyler waited in one of those rooms." She picked up a piece of oak trim that had once been attached to the back of the buffet. "I knew Mr. Harringer might hurt me, but I couldn't think of myself." She forced a chuckle. "Guess I'm a mama bear when it comes to my charges."

Susan shook her head. "I'll get a broom and dustpan for this dirt."

Regan watched Susan head down the hall where he remembered a utility closet held what she needed. He picked up a few more papers then plunged ahead. "Did the little girl's mother pick her up?"

"Her babysitter did, a high school girl," she replied. "The police visited with the girl and had me phone Leesa's mother at work. Mrs. Harringer was nearly hysterical, but an officer offered to escort the babysitter and Leesa home and stay with them until she arrived." Anita picked up the remainder of the ivy with one hand and the broken pottery with the other.

She always seems to carry too many loads. If she'd only allow Jesus to assume the role He once held in her heart. "What can I do?" Regan placed the last piece of paper on her desk.

"Nothing. I can finish cleaning this up."

"Not by yourself." He stood and righted the biggest portion of the buffet to its original position, but it leaned so precariously against the wall that he moved it to the back room. "I think a furniture restorer could mend this."

The phone rang again. While Anita dealt with the caller, Regan walked through the school, offering smiles and asking if any of them needed help. Anger simmered like a nest of angry yellow jackets. What kind of man bullied a woman, especially a woman in charge of a school full of small children? Craig needed to sit in jail for a long time, although Regan feared that wouldn't happen. Court orders could be issued and the security of the school tightened, but once Jacob Harringer arranged his son's release, nothing would stop Craig from creating havoc again. He'd escaped retribution for years.

Anita hung up the phone and eased into her chair. "This

father demanded I tell him immediately what went on today or he'd pull his son from the school."

"What did you tell him?" Regan asked.

"I have it handled! Just leave me alone," she said wearily. "I'll take care of this myself."

"I know you're upset." If he knew her better, he'd offer a shoulder or something.

"You have no idea what I'm feeling."

"You're right; I don't—"

"Then go on back to your fire-engine red Jeep and let me clean up my office. I don't need your help—any help."

seven

Anita tripped over a huge pillow in front of her TV and fell to her knees, cringing from the sting of a carpet burn. If Tyler hadn't been in bed, she'd have screamed at him to move the wretched thing. But what for? The pillow had taken up permanent residence on the floor for when they watched TV and played games.

I refuse to take out today's frustrations on my son.

She wanted to cry but felt too proud to break down, even in the privacy of her own home. Shedding tears in the aftermath of Vince's accident had been akin to breathing, but now she fought them with a vengeance. To make matters worse, fatigue needled at her body. She should go to bed and let this day slide under the covers of "best forgotten," now that everyone crowding her to rectify the disgusting matter with Craig Harringer had finally been handled. Since she'd arrived home from work, various staff members had phoned expressing their support, and a few parents who'd confiscated her home phone number had called insisting to know the whole story.

The parent letter explaining why policemen were summoned to school lay on the kitchen table ready to be copied in the morning. Pastor Miller approved her words and planned to be at the school in the morning to handle any emotional or questioning parents. His offer should have been a relief. For some reason, Pastor Miller intimidated her, yet he'd been nothing but kind and supportive since she came to Sweetwell. Not a word of criticism had poured from his mouth—only encouragement.

Frankly, after her handling of the situation today, the parents should feel even more secure about her directorship. Her actions demonstrated no one could pick up a child without the parents' express consent, and the letter conveyed those exact words.

Anita sighed and grabbed the pillow for a head rest. Guilt assaulted her conscience for the way she'd spoken to Regan. Her reasons for taking out her frustrations on him were nothing more than petty excuses linked to her fear of Craig Harringer. She needed to apologize. If she hadn't been so stubborn and proud, she could have used his help.

What time is it anyway? She'd left her watch by the kitchen sink while cleaning up from dinner. Forcing herself to stand, when in actuality she could have easily spent the night on the carpet, she shuffled across the room in search of her watch. Eleven. *Is it too late to call Regan?* How ungrateful she'd been, and he only meant to be a friend.

For a long moment, Anita toyed with the idea of calling him. Selfish as it sounded, if she didn't make amends tonight, she wouldn't catch a wink of sleep. Snatching up her cell phone, she punched in his number taped on the refrigerator. After three rings, she decided to hang up when he answered. His slurred words compounded her guilt.

"Oh, Regan, I'm so sorry. I shouldn't have called this late." Closing her eyes, she realized the nagging headache from earlier in the day had returned.

"Anita?"

"Yeah, I'll talk to you in the morning—"

"It's all right. Is something wrong?" His voice sounded anxious.

She released a pent-up breath. No wonder her shoulders were tight and her head pounded like a bass drum in a Fourth of July parade. "I simply need to apologize. As my mother says, I was spiteful this afternoon, and you were only trying to help."

"No problem. I understand bad days, and you had a real winner."

"I agree, but instead of thanking you, I tore into you like an angry dog."

"Rather me than one of your teachers or a parent."

She heard a smile in his voice and relaxed slightly. "It was no excuse for my rudeness." Silence invaded the moment. "Well, I'll let you get back to sleep."

"I'm wide awake. Is Tyler taking good care of you?"

She combed her fingers through her hair and walked to the sofa, settling down into its cushiony softness. "He's asleep and doesn't know a single thing about today. My mother keeps him after school, and she monitors everything."

"That's Theresa." He chuckled. "Nothing escapes her."

Knowing someone else appreciated her mother warmed her. "How long have you known Mom?"

"Since, oh, since the fire."

Great, now I've caused him to remember his family's death. "I didn't mean to bring up something painful."

"You didn't, not really," Regan instantly replied. "Your mother played the role of a substitute mom when I fell apart. I'll never forget what she did, never stop owing her. . . . See, my folks were on vacation then."

Mom's compassion must be why he took on Tyler. "Guess I owe her a lot too. She stayed with me for three months after the accident."

"Theresa has the gift of mercy with a healthy dose of optimism. She sees God's hand in everything."

Anita smiled, the first time all evening. She'd faked a grin or two for Tyler, because her thoughts had simply run wild with the day's happenings. "When I was a little girl, I wanted to be just like her when I grew up."

"And you are."

Startled, she weighed her words before answering. "I don't think so. I'm high strung, a perfectionist, and I love being in control. Mom's laid back and enjoys all life has to offer."

"I think you cut yourself short," Regan said with a yawn.

"You two are more alike than you think. The more I'm around you, the more I see the likeness."

Shaking her head, Anita attributed his comment to the lateness of the hour. She'd kept Regan on the phone much too long. "The time is getting away from me, and both of us need our rest. Thank you for accepting my apology. Sweet dreams and goodnight."

"I'll see you Saturday at Tyler's game."

The phone clicked in her ear. Saturday? So soon? Why did the thought of seeing him again twist at her insides like a tornado on a hot day? Did she want to see him. . .or not?

❧

The following morning, Anita met Susan in the preschool kitchen. The smell of brewing coffee waltzed around her senses—and Anita desperately needed a perk to begin her day. Sleep had come late with all the activities of the day twisting around her brain.

Today, before she permitted herself a cup of coffee, she'd copied letters for inquisitive parents and plenty more to stuff into children's tote bags. In twenty minutes, she'd be obliged to answer the phone. . .not a pleasant thought.

"Are you doing all right this morning?" Susan asked as the coffee finished dripping into the carafe.

"Yeah, thanks. I'll make it. The police picked up Craig Harringer last night, and Pastor Miller is stopping by to visit with parents this morning, sorta my backup support."

"Good. You need a pinch hitter today after that nasty business yesterday afternoon."

Anita opened the cupboard door in search of a granola bar, determined her friend would not see her still upset. "I agree. A couple of the parents were really obnoxious."

"Have you talked to Regan?" Susan asked.

Anita avoided her friend's meaningful stare. She knew exactly where the conversation was headed, and she'd really like a detour. "Yes, I called him last night."

Susan poured two cups of coffee. She handed Anita four sugar packets and two creamers. "Good. You weren't the picture of graciousness to him."

Oh, Susan. Regan is the last person I want to talk about this morning. "I know." Stirring her coffee, she watched it swirl in the cup, drowning the sugar crystals.

"He likes you." Susan took a sip of her black brew. "I can tell by the way he looks at you and the gentle sound of his voice."

"He's taken Tyler under his wing." Anita flicked an imaginary piece of dust from her blouse sleeve. "He thinks he can help him get rid of his nightmares."

"And how do you feel about it?"

"I'm not sure, but I'm willing to try. He's had enough tragedy of his own, and if nothing else, he has empathy for Tyler."

Susan's scrutiny poked at Anita's nerves. She knew it meant trouble.

"Out with it, Girlfriend," Anita said. "Your thoughts are louder than a room full of four year olds."

Her friend laughed. "Brushing up on our similes, are we?"

Anita leaned over to whisper. "I've known you since we shared bottles in the church nursery, and you're about to state something profound." She blew lightly on her coffee before taking a sip. The aroma equaled its rich, strong taste. "At least you'll think it's great."

"Possibly." Susan grinned. "I'll tell you what I see: Regan Moore's heart is ablaze for you. I can see the fire in his eyes."

"Oh, puh-leeze. You've been reading too many romance novels."

"Christian romance novels, thank you very much. And," Susan batted her eyes, "you rather like him."

"Absolutely not! Why, he grates at my nerves."

Her friend shrugged and took another long drink of coffee before moving toward the door. "We'll see. Why else did he come by the school yesterday? To put out a fire or to start one?"

Anita refused to reply. The rebuttal would only cause

Susan to continue her teasing.

"See, you know I'm right." She swung a gaze over her shoulder. "I didn't care much for Nick when I met him either, but then he started looking good—really good."

Laughing, Anita remembered Nick Walters in high school. "Susan, Nick had zits and weighed one hundred and twenty pounds soaking wet!"

She lifted her nose in pretended annoyance. "Love is blind, and after five years of marriage and two kids, he's the best thing that's happened to me since Jesus."

Watching her friend exit down the hall, leaving the scent of raspberry body splash in her wake, Anita didn't know whether to run after her for a hug or say nothing. She elected to root her feet firmly where they were planted.

Anita stood alone in the kitchen, allowing her mind to briefly dwell on yesterday afternoon's mishap. Frightening innocent children was the trait of a coward. But when Regan had walked through the front door, she'd felt relief wash over her. The truth rankled at her guarded heart. *Why, he can be insufferable. I don't need him. I'm not looking for or needing a relationship. I'm a mother and a professional who is happy and capable of living a single life.*

The understanding made her angry. Sweetwell's fire marshal had no business tampering with her emotions. He could kindle a romance with somebody else.

۞

The following Saturday morning's early soccer game seemed like an instant replay from the previous week. Again, Tyler stared anxiously at the parking lot during warm-ups until Regan's red Jeep pulled in beside her pearly white sedan. Immediately Tyler lifted his hand and waved more wildly than a flag caught in a gust of wind.

"Morning, Tyler," Regan called. "Looks like you're ready for a great game."

"You bet, Mr. Regan. Mom's over there," Tyler shouted.

Much to her dismay, the entire crowd heard her son's announcement. Some chuckled; others gawked like she'd been labeled their comic relief.

Anita cast her gaze to the field. She much preferred encouraging the team to being the center of gossip.

"Good mornin'." He handed her a small white sack from a donut shop. "Tyler said you liked the cream-filled ones."

Wonderful. Do you two always talk about me?

"Thank you." Notably, her stomach growled in response. She pulled the pastry from the sack and took a bite. "Hmm, this is perfect, vanilla pudding too."

"Better than just coffee?" A glint of mischief sparkled in his eyes.

"Absolutely. Where's yours?"

"Already ate it on the way here."

An uninvited smile tugged at her lips. "Was it licorice filled?" Suddenly she remembered the kiss Tyler had given her when he'd eaten the candy and how he'd asked Regan to give her one. Oh, how she wished she could bury her foolish remark.

Regan tossed a sideways grin. "They don't make licorice donuts, or I'd buy them out."

I don't have to talk to or pay any attention to him whatsoever. But the scent of his woodsy aftershave attacked her senses, and the smell was much more enticing than any donut. *I haven't been this confused in a long time.*

❧

Regan hadn't felt this confused in a long time. He groped for the right words to say to Anita, with the distinct feeling she'd rather be having her teeth pulled without anesthetic than be talking to him. In recompense, he concentrated on Tyler and the game, where his attention should have been in the first place. The thought of her being irked at him persisted.

"Have I upset you?" Her silence pushed him to distraction.

She neither looked his way nor flinched. "Of course not.

However did you get that idea?"

"You seem rather preoccupied."

"I'm watching my son's game."

What happened? I thought we were making headway.
Regan decided she must be a paradox: one minute she was
warm and friendly and the next a glacier.

When Tyler caught the ball before it sailed into the net
behind him, the crowd roared. Regan whistled and offered a
thumbs-up. From the corner of his eye, he could see Anita
jump and clap, reminding him of his high school days and
a certain pretty cheerleader. A wave of melancholy swept
over him. He'd married that pretty cheerleader.

They are nothing alike. After a moment's more delibera-
tion, he decided his deceased wife and Anita had nothing
more in common than the way in which they reacted to a
good play—and the fact that they'd both caught his eye. That
thought, though true, irritated him. Tyler, and Tyler alone,
needed his attention; anything else complicated his life.

"He's doing a great job," Regan said, his sights anchored
on the young boy.

"Oh, yes."

The excitement in her voice caused him to glance her way.
He noted the flushed cheeks and the way her eyes glistened.

"Were you a cheerleader?" he blurted out.

She issued an incredulous look. "Yes, I was."

"Thought so."

Her eyes widened. "Why? Do I look like I'm ready to turn
cartwheels?"

Precisely. "The idea crossed my mind."

For a minute, he thought she might pass on a piece of her
mind, then a half smile tweaked her lips. "It might embarrass
Tyler."

He jammed his hands into his pocket. "I think it might
entertain the crowd."

She turned her attention back to the field. "I wouldn't want to steal any of the attention from the team, now would I?"

Doesn't matter, because whether I like it or not, you have my attention. Dear Lord, help me before I fall so hard I bruise my heart.

eight

"Oh no, they lost," Anita groaned.

Tyler's shoulders could have swept the ground. She watched his teammates line up to shake their opponents' hands. When one of Tyler's friends cried, Anita wanted to run to the team's side and gather them into her arms.

"Kids this age shouldn't have to face defeat. They should simply be able to learn the game and have a good time." Regan watched the boys proceed through the line. "Look at those sad faces, as though their self-worth was measured by whether they win or lose."

Anita blinked back the tears, not because the team had lost, but because the boys were so disappointed. "I totally agree. I absolutely hate it when this happens."

"Stupid ref," one of the dads shouted. "Y'all called more penalties on us than them."

"He needs to be barred from the field," Regan muttered. "What is his attitude teaching the boys?"

"Nothing except to blame others when you don't succeed." Anita bit her tongue to keep from shouting at the man.

"We couldn't help that the goalie had slippery fingers," the same dad added.

Before Anita could tell the man exactly what she thought of his remark, Regan had stepped in front of him. "If you'd take the time to study the game, you'd see the ball has to go past every one of the other players before it gets to the goalie. It's not any more his responsibility than the rest of the team."

The man said nothing. He grabbed his folding chair and stomped away.

"I appreciate your words," Anita said when Regan joined

her. "I probably would have lost my temper."

"I nearly did." Regan released a labored sigh. "Ought to be something we can do for those little guys." He stared at the field. "Hmm, you know the coach is a friend of mine. I think I'd like to take the boys for hot chocolate and donuts. What do you think?"

All that sugar at nine-thirty in the morning? "I think they need to know they played well and winning is not everything. Guess a treat wouldn't hurt either."

He ambled toward where the coach had the boys seated on the grass. A few swiped at tears, Tyler included. Pausing, Regan whirled around and gave Anita his full attention. "Are you joining me?"

"Sure." *Do I really have a choice?*

❧

That same Saturday afternoon, while Anita vacuumed her living room and Tyler played in his room with a neighbor boy, a phone call from Rhonda Harringer interrupted her housework.

"Anita, I really need to talk to you about Leesa." Her voice sounded weak.

Immediately Anita assumed Craig had tried something again. Her spirits plummeted. Could he have been released from jail already? "Is Leesa okay?" Anita asked the girl's mother.

Rhonda burst into tears. "I think so. She still doesn't know what Craig did last Wednesday."

How hard this must be for you. "What can I do to help?"

The sound of Rhonda's sobs caused Anita's throat to constrict.

"He's out of jail," the woman finally said. "One more time, his dad bailed him out. Craig wasted no time in calling me and threatening to kidnap Leesa if I didn't allow him to see her."

"Did you contact the police?"

"Yes, but how can I prove he even called?" Rhonda paused, no doubt to gain control of her emotions. "I'm at my wit's end. I don't want to move from Sweetwell. This is our home, and I have a good job. I don't want to remove her from your school either. The education and Christian atmosphere at Good Hope cannot be equaled. But neither do I want Craig showing up again and causing problems. To top matters, my babysitter quit."

Surely he wouldn't try the same stupid stunt again. "I'm not worried about him making a return visit." Anita hoped her words didn't convey her true feelings. Just the thought of the man made her shiver. "He could go to jail for a very long time, especially since I filed assault charges against him."

"I don't think he's afraid of jail. He thinks he's immune to the law—probably because his family's money has always paid for his mistakes."

"Rhonda, I'll do whatever I can. Has a trial date been set?"

"Yes, but not for about two months."

"Do you have a good lawyer?"

Silence prevailed, sending a gloomy message. "Due to my limited income, I had to settle on a court-appointed attorney."

Oh, no. "Some of them have excellent reputations. They care about their clients and do a great job."

"Not mine." Rhonda's words echoed with finality.

Anita felt as though someone had punched her in the stomach. She neither knew what to say nor how to comfort the hurting woman. "I wonder if the church has an attorney among its members?"

"I wouldn't know," Rhonda said with a sigh. "I don't attend Good Hope; mine is a small church outside of town."

"I could ask Pastor Miller to see if he could recommend someone."

"But I couldn't afford—"

"The church is full of good people who want to help. If there's a person who can assist you, he'll find out. I'm sure the fees would be negotiable. Christians are loving people, Rhonda." *Am I actually promoting the church?* Then she remembered the kindness Pastor Miller and the preschool board had exhibited during last week's problem.

"Do you really think so?"

"I'm positive." And Anita knew without a doubt she believed every word. Although she couldn't quite label her belief as faith, she recalled a time when she had.

"Can we talk more on Monday morning?"

"Why don't you bring Leesa a few minutes early? Maybe I'll have some news for you."

"Thanks. . .thanks for everything."

The phone clicked in Anita's ear. *I sure made a quick commitment. Asking Pastor Miller about a lawyer within the church?* She hadn't stretched herself like this in years.

Was it improper to call the pastor at home? After all, he'd told her to call anytime.

Already she regretted this involvement in the Harringer feud. The courts would sort this mess and take care of Craig harassing Rhonda and anyone else who got into his way. *But I'm already knee-deep in this dilemma.*

Shaking her head, she phoned Pastor Miller. This would be the end of it.

≈

The next morning, with Tyler nestled between her and her mother, Anita attempted to focus on the worship service instead of the zillion and one matters racing through her mind. If it hadn't been for her mother's insistence upon church attendance, she'd be home catching up on sleep or organizing the next week of school.

Shifting in her seat, she recalled her phone conversation with the pastor on Saturday afternoon. He hoped to have an attorney's name for her this morning, possibly even arrange a meeting. It seemed a lawyer from Good Hope, a Patrick somebody, might be willing to take on representing Rhonda. Anita had no choice but to pack a pew and feign concentration on the service.

Tyler gave her a wink and looked up from the Bible puzzle given to all the children when they entered the sanctuary. He'd completed the dot-to-dot of Moses carrying the stone-carved Ten Commandments.

"Very good," she whispered in his ear. On the other side of the page was a maze about the Israelites wandering through the desert in search of the Promised Land. Anita pointed to it and nodded for him to go ahead. *They wandered for forty years going nowhere physically or spiritually. I'm working on three.*

Pastor Miller's words gripped her attention. "Just as God took care of the Israelites by providing manna each morning for them to eat, He promises to meet our needs. His plan for us may not be what we envision, but His plan is perfect."

Vince's accident couldn't be part of a perfect plan. Give me a break. What about giving Tyler what he needs? A father? Someone to teach him all those things a man shares with his son? Someone to love him? Hold him? Play ball? No, thanks. I don't buy any of that. The best around here is the Big Brother program, and it's no substitute for a real dad.

❧

Regan glanced across the aisle and up a row of pews to where Anita sat with her small family. A myriad of emotions crept across her face. He saw a blank stare change from sadness to sweet tenderness with Tyler, then to anger. Could the pastor's message cause such intense feelings?

How wonderful to think she might be making a rededication to the Lord. But he honestly had no clue what thoughts danced through her head. He'd given up on understanding her and accepted he couldn't read or predict her reactions to anything. Just when he believed he might be gaining ground in the arena of friendship, she'd run to the woods without leaving a trail. Tracking wasn't one of his fortes. He had a hard enough time eliminating potential fires.

Conscious of allowing his mind to drift during Pastor Miller's sermon, Regan pulled his thoughts back to focus on the message. God did meet all his needs, even during those difficult months after the fire. When Regan searched to find himself after all the long weeks of grieving, he found God waiting and ready to help him heal. *Sure glad I didn't have to wander forty years before I understood God's love—although at the time it felt that long.*

Once the pastor had dismissed the congregation, Regan looked for Anita and Tyler. He'd been caught up with friends and hadn't seen them leave the sanctuary. Glancing about the foyer for the freckle-faced boy and his willowy mother, Regan spied them with Pastor Miller. He sauntered over to say good morning and invite Anita and Tyler to lunch, despite the fact he wondered why on earth he wanted lunch with such an unpredictable woman.

Patrick Montgomery, a single lawyer, stood between Anita and the pastor. The sight stopped Regan from taking another step. *Maybe she's interested in him.*

"Patrick, I'd like for you to meet Anita Todd," Pastor Miller said. "She's the woman I told you about."

The lawyer smiled warmly and grasped her hand. "Good to meet you. The pastor has told me all about your circumstances, and I'm eager to help."

"Thank you, and it's a pleasure to meet you too. From everything the pastor has said, sounds like you're perfect."

Perfect for what? What does she see in him? How could he be a positive influence on Tyler?

Patrick laughed. "Not exactly, but I can see we'll get along just fine."

A woman called to Pastor Miller. "Excuse me," he said to the couple. "I have another pressing matter here. Since I put you two together, guess you don't need me. Anita, call me if you need anything."

"Thank you."

Patrick bent down to Tyler. "How are you?"

"Good, Sir," Tyler replied.

The lawyer stood and faced Anita. "Shall I call you this afternoon or in the morning at school?"

"This afternoon would be better." Anita flashed him an incredibly sweet smile.

Tyler turned around and saw Regan. "Hi, Mr. Regan."

The term invisible suddenly held new meaning. "Hi, Tyler." He glanced at Anita. "Good morning."

She returned the gesture, but her gaze refused to meet his. "Regan, do you know Patrick Montgomery?"

"Yes, I do. Good to see you again." Regan reached to shake the lawyer's hand.

He is a great guy—and probably good for Anita and Tyler.

"Mr. Regan is a fire marshal," Tyler said with an air of importance. "And he used to be a real fireman."

"Wow, that's impressive," Patrick said.

Regan felt noticeably uncomfortable. "Well, I didn't mean to interrupt, just wanted to say good morning." He gave Patrick his attention. "Have a good afternoon."

"I have soccer practice on Tuesday," Tyler offered, grinning through his missing front teeth.

"I'll be there, Sport." Regan ruffled the boy's dark, curly hair before snatching another look at Anita.

"We'll arrange something," she said to Regan. Her professionalism oozed from every word. She wore a light blue suit, giving her a very classy look.

He forced a smile and walked away. *Patrick doesn't look like her type. Her type? How would I know her type? I barely know her. What's wrong with me?* Regan stepped out into the warm fall day. He loosened his tie and scanned the parking lot for his Jeep, although he knew exactly where he'd parked it—same place every Sunday.

I'm jealous. I can't believe this. I ought to be swatted with the nearest limb.

nine

By Tuesday morning, Anita began to wonder why she hadn't heard from Regan. Not that she really cared, or did she? Tyler had asked about him at breakfast, reminding her about soccer practice and Regan's assurance that he planned to be there. Certainly her concerns centered on her son. He'd be crushed if Regan decided to stop his involvement with the Big Brother program.

I just want everything to be right for Tyler. Nothing else. Regan had his friendlier moments. Once he climbed down off his high horse, he could be fun. After all, Tyler adored him.

With a shrug, she settled into the morning's routine: returning phone calls, scheduling field trips, and checking over the cook's budget for snacks.

Anita paused to take a long look outside the eight-foot-long window of her office. A day had crept into view as brilliant as she could remember. Oak trees, older than the town, feathered green against a cloudless blue sky. Their branches waved lightly in the lambent light as if welcoming her to join them. White impatiens nestled in the oaks' shade, lifting their faces to take refuge from the sun's fast approaching heat. A paintbrush assortment of black-eyed Susans, bright blue salvia, and pink mums bloomed against the backdrop of a white picket fence lining the front walk of the school. The color contrast sent tingles to her toes in a mixture of awe and admiration, as though God had labored over His creation like an artist deliberately brushing colors on a canvas.

Here I am giving God credit for His handiwork while I'm mad at Him. Oh, God, I know how beautiful Your creation is, but taking Vince and plaguing Tyler with nightmares is cruel.

Why? What have I done—or my son—to deserve this misery?

Anita blinked and turned her attention to the paperwork on her desk. Someday she needed to deal with all these things, but not today. Only on Sundays did the overwhelming desire to once more draw near to God tug at her heart.

The phone rang, jarring her from her musing. She shivered and hastily picked it up on the second ring.

"Hi, Anita. It's Regan. Is this a good time?"

She felt her burdens fade in light of his call. "Now is fine. What's going on in the world of our fire marshal?"

He chuckled—the familiar low mirth that seemed to originate in his toes. "The same paperwork and occasional inspection. I wanted to make sure it was okay to pick up Tyler for soccer practice this evening."

She detected a slight chill in his voice. "Is something wrong?"

"No. Just busy here today."

"Oh, okay. Well, you can pick him up the same time as last week. I know he's looking forward to seeing you."

"Good. Me too. Do you mind if we catch dinner?"

"No problem. Hey, what if I have dessert when you get back?"

"That sounds great." His voice inched more enthusiastic.

"What about an Italian wedding cake?" *Now why did I suggest that?*

"What. . .are you proposing?" He chuckled again, and she smiled through her humiliation.

"A cake, Mr. Moore. It's a creamy white concoction."

"Ah. I thought you had something else in mind, a little more permanent. I've never been proposed to. Sounds interesting."

Anita felt her face burn. *I walked into this round.*

Regan laughed again. "Do I have the lady speechless?"

"No, I'm simply thinking." The phone indicated another call. "Got to run, the other line is ringing."

"Saved by the bell, huh? I'll see you later. Wouldn't miss your cake for the world."

Anita replaced the receiver, so glad no one else occupied the front office. She could almost hear Susan teasing her about the caller who reddened her face.

For a moment, she dared to prop her elbow on the desk and rest her chin on her hand. She rather liked Regan Moore in a peculiar sort of way. A twinge of alarm raced through her at this realization. How many times did she have to tell herself a relationship did not fit into her carefully laid plans? *A friend, he's simply a friend.*

After school, she picked up Tyler at her mother's and made a quick stop at the grocery. She didn't have buttermilk, coconut, pecans, or cream cheese for the cake and frosting.

"Need a cart, Mom?" Tyler asked. "I can push it."

She hesitated. "Probably so. We just need four things, but you know me when I get around food."

"And we're both a little hungry, so you might want to buy more stuff."

My sweet little rascal. "So what kind of snack would you like? I could get us some bananas."

"How about grapes?"

Anita smiled. "Green ones? Those that don't have seeds?"

"Sure, Mom. Can I pick them out?"

She guided him to the fruit section where the scent of oranges caused her stomach to growl. She tossed a couple of the huge navel beauties into a plastic bag and set them in the cart. While she perused the fresh produce, the sound of thunder accompanied by a waterfall indicated the vegetables were receiving their timely shower—all designed to keep them garden fresh and appetizing. Her gaze moved to the tomatoes where droplets of water sent a silent message of, "Buy me; I'm home grown." She did.

Together, Anita and Tyler moved on to collect the ingredients for the cake, ending up in the dairy section.

"B-u-t-t-e-r-m-i-l-k," Tyler spelled, holding the quart container in his hand. He peered up at her, obviously confused.

"What kind of milk is this? Yellow?"

"No, Honey." She hugged his shoulders and planted a kiss on his upturned nose. "Buttermilk is the type of milk left after butter is churned. Your granddad used to love it."

"Would I?" His serious look nearly made her laugh.

"I doubt it. You have to develop a taste for it."

"Like yogurt?"

If you only knew. "Something like that."

"Anita Todd?"

She whirled around at the sound of her name. Instantly the blood rushed from her face and her stomach churned. Craig Harringer.

&

Regan read through a suspected arson case. Ordinarily, he stuck to his job, conducting inspections for fire code violations and administrating and enforcing the fire code for the state of Oklahoma. In larger cities, his position also utilized an aide, but not in Sweetwell. Here he did it all.

This case piqued his interest because it involved a prominent family in the community—the Harringers—and he wasn't so sure the blaze had been accidental.

His approach to fires had always been suspicious and cautious until a cause had been established. Whether the fire originated from an electrical malfunction, a careless cigarette, or kids playing with matches, every one had a cause. Period. Regan needed to put this blaze into one of three categories: accidental, an act of God, or incendiary.

No matter how many times he pushed the memory of his wife and daughter into the back of his mind or prayed for God to take away the horror of finding their charred bodies, fire was his enemy. He believed the memory of his wife and daughter kept him committed to fire safety—a way of preventing others from suffering through the loss of life. By concentrating on those worthwhile thoughts, he could see how God uses sorrow for good. Others could be helped, taught, and instructed about fire prevention and thereby escape tragedy. The arsonist who fell under Regan's scrutiny had better be ready to run.

Glancing through the first-in firefighter's report, Regan read the answers to the standard questions. A policeman had reported the blaze while patrolling the area around eleven o'clock. Neither the officer nor first-arriving firefighter saw anyone near the warehouse or while they battled the blaze. Thick, black smoke poured from the building, leaving the impression that the area housed large quantities of consumer packaged flammable liquids—turpentine, lacquer thinner, and paint solvent—in metal gallon containers. *This must be the origin.*

Monday night's blaze would not be an easy fire to determine the cause, and oddly enough, neither the burglar nor the fire alarm systems had sounded a warning. Regan reread a note on the final firefighter's report—office window broken and a crowbar found inside. Looked like forced entry. He could kick himself for not seeing this earlier. In his mind, it definitely spelled arson.

Regan had mixed feelings about Jacob and Doris Harringer, somewhere between pity and total frustration. They supported the community and gave freely to various charities, but Regan wouldn't give a wooden nickel for Craig, their only son. The incident at Good Hope Christian Day School cemented his opinion.

Jacob owned the now burned warehouse complex outside of town—one of his many investments. Everything had been constructed according to the building code. Farther down the report, Regan read that six months ago Craig had been given ownership to the building, and the construction was handsomely insured. *This sounds even worse.*

Craig had a record with the police department long enough to name a cell after him. He'd always been a hothead in his teens and had never grown up, just gotten worse. Jacob's money kept him in alcohol and drugs, then went on to pay legal fees so Craig wouldn't have to sit in jail. Hence the problem: Craig seldom if ever faced the consequences of his actions. The elder Harringer mistook love for providing his son everything he demanded.

The town thought Craig had finally grown up when he married Rhonda, a great lady who moved to Sweetwell without prior knowledge of Craig's past.

He got drunk and beat her a few times, but when she called the police and filed charges, Jacob again bailed his son out of trouble. Rhonda and Craig tried for reconciliation when she became pregnant, but his change of heart didn't last once their little girl made it to eight months old. He must have grown tired of Rhonda, because he filed for divorce based on mental anguish. Jacob's money paid for a fancy lawyer out of Tulsa in an effort to gain custody of Leesa, but the courts denied Craig those privileges when he lost his temper in front of the judge. A series of assaults on Rhonda pulled the plug on any visitation at all.

What puzzled Regan was why Craig might have started the warehouse fire. He didn't need money. Jacob held the purse strings, but he'd never refused his son—although at the last trial when Rhonda had showed up with a broken arm and a bruised face, Jacob had walked out and left his son to face the consequences. When the judge gave him ninety days, Craig served two weeks. Jacob couldn't handle knowing his son was behind bars.

Regan stole a quick look at his watch. He had plenty of time this afternoon to do a little investigating of his own before heading to Tyler's soccer practice. The thought of Anita and her energetic son were all the more reason to nail Craig with an arsonist charge. The man shouldn't have threatened Anita, her staff, or any of those children at Good Hope School.

Regan drove to the site about a half-mile out of town and

parked his Jeep beside the ruins of Harringer's Warehouse. Snatching up his hand-held recorder, camera, and a small bag with a few tools, he stuffed them into a backpack and headed for what was left of the building. Although the fire had originated in the area housing the flammable liquids, he needed to determine the exact cause.

Regan knew this initial investigation would be limited to recording his essential findings and photographing. He had a lot of work ahead of him, some of which could be done when a deputy from the office of the State Fire Marshal's office assigned to Sweetwell arrived on Thursday. Usually this type of work concluded quickly, but not in the case of arson.

ૐ

"What do you want?" Anita asked Craig. She sensed Tyler right beside her, and her stomach curdled. "Honey, why don't you get us some vanilla ice cream to go with the cake tonight? You know which brand."

He scampered off to the frozen food aisle. At that point, she didn't care if he came back with a dozen ice-cream containers.

Narrowing her gaze at Craig, she repeated her question.

"Do I need a reason?" His half smile more closely resembled a sneer. "Aren't we friends?"

"Not exactly. Look, I have things to do." Anita scrutinized his designer jeans and expensive pullover. Those clothes didn't mask the man beneath—the violence she knew could erupt at any given moment. To think her initial impression of him centered on his charm and good looks.

"I won't forget you wouldn't let me have my daughter," he said in a low voice.

Anita refused to cower to his threats. She glanced around her at the rows of yogurt, butter, and milk on one side and the various cheeses on the other. An older couple stopped for milk and argued over skim or two percent. *Can't you see I need help!*

"I don't have to listen to your threats," she said, loud

enough for the couple to hear. Instead of intervening, they moved on down the aisle, obviously thinking they'd interrupted a marital quarrel. Anita started to push the cart past Craig, but he grabbed it.

"You'll regret calling the police that day," he uttered barely above a whisper. "I don't take kindly to folks interfering with my business."

She swallowed hard. "I don't regret what I did, and I'd do it again. Maybe the next time you'll sit in jail a little longer."

He nodded, and scorn covered every inch of his face. "Nice looking boy you have there, Mrs. Todd."

ten

Paralyzed by fear, Anita watched Craig disappear down the aisle, around the corner, and out of view. Every ounce of strength from the core of her being emptied itself into a puddle of sheer terror. She gripped the handles of the shopping cart as though clinging to some semblance of hope. Reality had erected its nasty head and struck its poisonous venom into her lifeblood.

Craig's final words repeatedly hammered into her brain. *Nice looking boy you have there, Mrs. Todd.*

His threat would never hold up in a court of law—not even to a police officer. How could a man get away with the crimes he'd committed against innocent people?

"Mom, Mom."

Somewhere in the recesses of her tremulous thoughts, Anita heard Tyler calling her name. She drew in a deep breath and found herself desperately trying to respond.

"Mom, Mom."

She blinked. Her wrists ached from her hold on the cart. *My son.* "Yes, Honey."

"Are you okay? I mean, Mom, you look sick. Lemme have your cell phone, and I'll call Grandma."

She took the ice cream from his hands and resisted the urge to hold him close. "I'm fine. Let's hurry so we can have our snack before soccer practice."

He stepped in front of the cart. "I'll push. You don't need to worry about anything when I'm with you."

She inhaled deeply and held her breath to keep from bursting into tears. She seldom cried—saw no reason for it. What should she do? She couldn't approach an officer without endangering the safety of her son. For a moment, she wondered if Craig might be waiting in the parking lot to follow her.

Anita paid the cashier, and she and Tyler made their way to their car. In what she hoped was a casual manner, she glanced around the parking lot, looking for signs of Craig Harringer. She didn't see him, but that didn't ease her worries.

If only Tyler didn't have soccer practice tonight. She preferred not to let him out of her sight. All the while he was gone, her mind would race with the what-ifs, and she'd pace the floor until he returned. The idea of staying at the field with Regan seemed her only choice. She'd gladly abandon the cake idea.

"Mom, I can't wait for your cake." Tyler locked the car doors and buckled his seat belt. "It's my favorite you know."

"I know." She stuck the key into the ignition. "What if I make it another time and I tag along to your practice?"

Tyler wrinkled up his nose. "Aw, Mom. This is the guy's night. Ya know? Just me and Mr. Regan."

Please, Honey. "You don't want me there?"

He shook his head. "Are you mad at me?"

"Of course not." If she didn't gain control now, she'd be blinded in tears. Regan. She could trust him.

ತಿ

Regan watched Tyler's team form two lines for drills. The boys would then kick-pass back and forth, with each boy taking his turn then running to the end of the line to repeat. Normally the scramble to make contact with the ball and successfully maneuver it to the opposite side brought a lot of inward chuckles; six year olds often lost sight of what they were supposed to do. Some simply couldn't make contact with the ball, and some easily pursued one distraction or another. But this evening Regan's mind centered on Tyler's nightmares. They hadn't talked about his bad dreams, and Regan pondered whether to bring up the matter or wait. He'd prayed for patience, desiring to win the boy's confidence before delving into the abyss of his young mind. It might take weeks, even months, before Tyler finally spoke about his problem, and possibly longer before he allowed Regan to venture into his nightmare world. He wondered if the boy had suffered through another one lately. One way to find out.

He pulled his phone from his jeans pocket and punched in the code for Anita's number. She had acted strangely when she dropped Tyler off, distracted and decidedly pale.

"You'll stay right there with him, won't you?" she'd asked, obviously shaken.

"He won't be out of my sight. Are you okay?"

"I'm. . .I'm fine. Do you mind calling me when you go eat?"

"You have my word." He wanted to talk to her longer, but Tyler was anxious to get to practice.

Now, when she answered her cell, Regan heard the strain in her voice. "Anita, are you all right?"

"Not exactly. I have a few things on my mind."

"Can I help? I'm good at putting out fires." He waited to hear her light giggle, but nothing came. "That serious, huh?"

"Very." Another long moment passed. "Is Tyler on the field?"

"Yes, there isn't a soul for miles, and I haven't taken my eyes off him. So please tell me what's wrong."

"This will stay between us, no matter what I tell you?" Her voice, though soft, held the strands of panic.

He waited a moment more, weighing her words and trying to read what her emotions relayed. "I want to help. Sounds like you're in trouble. Does this have anything to do with Craig Harringer? Or Tyler?"

"Both. Craig threatened me today." She proceeded to tell Regan all that had transpired at the grocery, leaving nothing out. "I wanted to come with you two tonight, but Tyler didn't seem to care for the idea."

How dare that man bully a woman? Seems to be a habit with him. Rage raced through him while a picture of Anita and Tyler with Craig towering over them clung to his mind.

He remembered the atrocities Craig had committed against Rhonda, and she was his wife and the mother of his child!

The arson case from the afternoon had aroused an old vengeance against the fire monster, and now a threat to Anita and Tyler clawed at his heart. Craig Harringer's degradation knew no boundaries.

Despair, Regan understood. Craig had chosen the one sure way to get to Anita—through Tyler. Like every mother, she'd stop at nothing to ensure her child's well-being.

Craig, the clever snake. He'd gambled on Anita relinquishing her responsibilities at the school so he could take Leesa.

"I don't know what to do," she finally said. "I can't let him take Leesa from the school, but I'm so afraid for Tyler. I shouldn't be forced to make a decision like this, should I?" She sounded weak, helpless.

"Not at all. Let me do some thinking about the proper way to approach the police—"

"No! He'll hurt Tyler."

He ached to comfort her, assure her everything could be worked out. "We can't let him get away with this. Keep your door locked. I have Tyler, and Craig knows better than to cross my path. We'll talk later, but in the meantime, would you like for me to pray with you?"

"No, not really. I don't think it would help. God left me to fend for myself over two years ago."

I understand your misery, but He is the answer. "Anita, He loves you. I admit we get frustrated when we don't understand His ways, but He has a plan—"

"Nothing good," she interrupted, "can come from Vince's death, Tyler's nightmares, and this psycho threatening a six year old. The God I met as a child was a loving and merciful being. The God I found as an adult has done nothing but hurt me time and time again, along with my son."

Oh, Lord, how can I make her understand? "I'd do anything to see your faith restored, because I've been where you are."

She sighed, and he wondered if tears had overcome her. "And when did the world start looking better? I mean did you wake up one morning and suddenly feel God loved you again? The deaths in your family didn't matter?"

The anguish he sensed eating at her soul moved him to silently pray as he answered her. "My healing didn't happen overnight. God didn't give up on me, and He won't give up on you either." He wished he could hold her. "This isn't the time to talk about these things. I'd rather we talk face-to-face, but for right now, rest assured that Tyler is fine, and he's safe with me."

"Thank you," she whispered.

"Do you want me to bring him straight home or have dinner first?"

"I'm not sure. I'm scared out of my wits." She paused. "I have this cake nearly done."

"Why did you bother with baking after what happened?"

She sighed. "To keep my mind occupied."

I've been there, anything so you don't have to think. "Why don't I pick up some subs, and we can eat at the apartment?"

"Do you mind?"

"Not at all. We'll bring you one too. Just tell me what you'd like. . ." *This is simply too much for her to bear alone.*

A moment later, Regan replaced his phone and tried without success to focus on the remainder of the practice. Craig Harringer had just catapulted himself to the top of Regan's most-wanted-behind-bars list.

Oh, Lord, show Anita Your perfect love. Give her the peace that only comes from You. You know better than I what she's feeling, but I do know she needs a fresh touch of Your Spirit. And Lord, keep Your eyes on Tyler.

≈

"Are you too full to tackle this cake, Sport?" Regan asked Tyler. The boy had eaten a meatball sandwich, pickles, and chips, and drunk a tall glass of milk.

"Not my mom's cake." Tyler's chocolate-colored eyes sparkled. "Wait 'till you taste it."

"Anita, what's this called again?"

She laughed, allowing the light-hearted conversation to momentarily soothe her worries. "Italian wedding cake."

"Ah, yes, now I remember. Does it come with a proposal?"

Tyler glanced at Regan, then at Anita. "What's a proposal?"

Regan cleared his throat and pointed his fork at Tyler, as though poised to teach him an invaluable concept. "A proposal is when a man asks a woman to spend the rest of her life with him. If she says yes, then they get married."

Tyler nodded and stuck his fork into a small slice of cake, snatching up a large dollop of frosting. "Why don't you and Mom get married? Sounds like a good idea to me."

Anita wanted to disappear into the woodwork. Where in the world did her precious son come up with these ideas?

Regan laughed heartily. "Most people who get married spend a lot of time getting to know each other, then fall in love before the proposal."

Just as she had taught him, the little boy swallowed his bite of cake before he spoke. "No problem. Mom's pretty cool, and she's kinda pretty. I like her cooking too."

Again Anita couldn't believe her ears. "Let's talk about something else."

Regan's eyes twinkled. "I like this topic, but what did you have in mind?"

She gave him an "enough" look before passing a sweet smile onto Tyler. "What about a game of fish after you finish your cake and have your bath?"

"Sure." Tyler dragged out the word.

"Don't forget to brush your teeth. And after the game, off to bed without a peep, okay?"

He nodded and grinned at Regan. "See, she's not so bad. I bet you could get used to taking a bath every day and doing chores. I have to keep my room clean and empty the trash, but yours could be different."

"Tyler." Anita's voice rose. Why didn't he ever voice embarrassing statements when they were alone? She couldn't even look at Regan, and she certainly didn't need a mirror to tell her that her face bordered on crimson.

Regan chuckled and stabbed his fork into a generous hunk of cake. Anita fumed, and when she caught his gaze, he winked.

"What kind of chores?" he whispered when Tyler left the table to put his plate and fork into the sink.

"Hush. Can't you see I'm absolutely mortified?"

"Sure can. You wear red quite well."

While Tyler took his bath, Regan helped Anita clean up from dinner. Once the teasing about Tyler's innocent remarks ended, her spirits plummeted. For a short hour, she'd forgotten about Craig Harringer.

"I can tell by the look on your face what's going on in that pretty head of yours," Regan said.

His words were sweet, caring, and she didn't mind he'd ventured further into their friendship—not really. She nodded and swiped at an unbidden tear. "I'm afraid."

He wiped the wetness from her cheek with his finger. She stared at the sink filled with the remains from dinner, ready to be ground into the garbage disposal. At that moment, she felt like the discarded food—useless and at the mercy of an angry man.

"Anita."

She peered into his face, but then more tears pooled her eyes. *I don't believe in crying; it doesn't solve a thing.* "Yes," she managed.

"You can get a protective order."

"Isn't it the same as a restraining order?"

He placed his hand over hers. Any other time, any other man, she'd have recoiled, but her heart ached for comfort. "Not exactly. A restraining order is a civil process and cannot be enforced by the police. Violating a protective order involves criminal matters."

"Do you recommend it?"

Regan pressed his lips firmly together. "Yes, I do. Patrick could file it for you, and it lets Craig know you mean business. He can be arrested with the slightest violation such as harassing you or Tyler."

She nodded. The thought had crossed her mind earlier. "Do you really believe it will stop him?"

He swallowed hard. "Honestly, with Harringer's record, I don't know if anything short of having him behind bars would deter him. It's like a speed bump and a red light."

"I thought so. As long as he's out of jail, he's capable of anything."

"I don't think he's so stupid as to deliberately ruin his chances for visitation with his daughter."

"But what about Rhonda? Look at the times he's hurt her. It's no use. I can't stop him, and neither will a piece of paper, but. . .I will call Patrick." Her throat tightened in an effort to ward off the tears.

"He's an excellent attorney."

"Must be why Pastor Miller recommended him for Rhonda. She told me all she could afford was a court-appointed one, so I asked the pastor if he could make a recommendation—that's when he introduced me to Patrick."

He rubbed the back of his neck, as though uncomfortable about something. "Rhonda needs all the help she can get."

"What frightens me the most is Craig is desperate, which means he's capable of anything. Mom and Rhonda told me vicious things about him."

"Then we'll have to be one step ahead of him." He leaned against the doorway.

"This afternoon I called Tyler's school and spoke to the principle and his teacher." Her shoulders ached. In fact, her whole body hurt to the ends of her toes. "I didn't tell them anything except no one but Mom could ever pick him up. Of course they told me state laws wouldn't permit anyone else to take him from school property."

"Good girl." The soft tone of his voice soothed her in a way she didn't understand, but appreciated.

She took a deep breath and attempted to sound light. "You should have heard Mom when I told her about what happened at the grocery."

"I can only imagine"

"She said she had a baseball bat for creeps like him, and she wouldn't hesitate to use it." She remembered her mother's animated gestures. "You know how she can get wound up."

Regan offered a smile. "You can be sure Tyler is safe with her."

Anita refused to look at Regan for fear she'd step into his arms and sob. *I can't break down. I have to be strong for Tyler.* She refused to give the impression of a weak woman, unable to handle her own problems. She'd made it through worse. . . .

"Let yourself cry," he urged, stepping closer.

"No." She shook her head. "Tyler might see, and I must keep my mind clear. He doesn't know about today."

The bathroom door opened, and Tyler stepped out dressed in his Oklahoma State football pajamas and looking sleepy. "What story are you going to read me tonight, Mom? I think I'll pass on the fish game."

Anita struggled to regain her composure and moved from the kitchen into the hallway. She'd almost given in to the shelter of Regan's arms. *Put on a smile, Girl. You're a supermom.* "What would you like to hear?"

Tyler touched his forefinger to his chin. "Could Mr. Regan read to me?"

She had to bite her tongue to ward off the pain coursing through her body. She knew he adored Regan and wanted every minute of the man's time. "We have lots of new books from the library I could read—"

"Please, since we're not playing the game."

How selfish of her to tell him no. "Sure." She smiled and turned to Regan. "He's all yours."

Regan's glance revealed his compassion. "Sport, I don't want to take away from you and your mom's special time. We've had all evening together."

"Please, Mr. Regan."

She nodded at the man, silently urging him to comply with her son's wishes.

"Tell you what, Sport. What if I tell you a story? I've got a pretty good one about strangers. In fact you can help me tell it."

Oh God, if You are there, I thank You. And if You have any feelings for Tyler, please protect him. He's all I have left.

eleven

Regan reread the Harringer warehouse fire notes. He'd typed his investigative report from his tape recorder and printed out the pictures from his digital camera. The only fact he knew for sure was the point of origin, but the mystery still lay in the cause.

The main office had not fully burned, which allowed him to inspect the closet door housing the burglar and fire alarm systems. It seemed a bit peculiar for the arsonist to use a crowbar to gain access to the closet, then leave it there for the firefighters to find. Too simple, too easy. But the entry had allowed him to disconnect the wires to both systems.

Regan refused to list the cause of the fire as undetermined. By the time he finished probing through the remains, the arsonist had better be ready to confess or take the next flight out of the country.

Scrolling down his list of phone numbers on his personal digital assistant, Regan found Patrick Montgomery's number. While he waited for the lawyer's office to answer, he closed the door with his foot. No point in anyone else hearing the conversation. How stupid he'd felt when he'd learned Anita and Patrick's relationship was business related—and for Rhonda's sake. Good thing he hadn't made a fool of himself that Sunday after church when he saw them together. Shaking his head, Regan listened for Patrick's secretary to put him through.

"Patrick, Regan Moore here. I've been thinking we might help each other in a mutual venture."

"How's that?"

"By swapping a bit of information about a certain friend of ours."

"And who are we talking about?"

"Craig Harringer."

"Keep talking." Regan heard the man's chair turn. Obviously he had the attorney's attention.

"You know his warehouse burned night before last, and I intend to announce arson in the morning."

"Interesting."

"Forced entry with a crowbar. One of the firefighters found it. Now someone could be holding a grudge against our buddy, or he might have had a hand in it himself. What puzzles me is his father holds the purse strings, but he's always untied them the moment Craig squealed money. I don't see why Craig would be pressed for money with Jacob always there to hand out more."

"Except Jacob isn't fueling Craig's pockets anymore."

Regan chuckled at Patrick's choice of words. "Since when?"

"Since Rhonda took him to court this last time. When Craig beat her so badly she needed hospitalization, Jacob walked out of the courtroom."

"I'd heard rumors about that but didn't know for sure." Regan tapped his pen on the desktop. "Interesting."

"You stole my line." This time Patrick laughed. "Truth is, Craig's broke. Blown every penny."

Motive.

"Do you suppose Jacob would talk to me?" Patrick asked.

"I doubt it. He threatened to sic his Doberman on me the last time I paid a call. So what are you thinking?"

"Oh. . .probably the same thing you are."

Regan dropped his pen. "I'll keep in touch. Talk to you soon." He replaced the handset and stared wistfully out the window. Hard to believe September had come to Oklahoma with its still hot temps but a promise of cooler days to come. Kind of like his mood with the suspected arson and his concerns for Rhonda, Anita, and Tyler. The possibility of playing a round of golf nudged at him, a way of escape from the questions plaguing his mind. If only he didn't have so much work to do—and so much of it had to do with Craig Harringer. With charges against him for his actions at Good Hope School and possibly an arson charge too—well, he could be sitting in prison for quite awhile. *Couldn't think of a better person to utilize the taxpayer's money.*

Resting his feet atop a stack of papers and files, Regan stared outside and let his mind drift with Craig's scenario. Without Jacob's money, he couldn't pay legal fees or his bills. Those circumstances led to one desperate man. He wondered if Craig would offer a rebuttal to the arson announcement in the morning. Of course he might choose to volunteer his help or give a few names of those who opposed him, which would make him look innocent.

I need to determine the cause of the fire, then check alibis. Glancing at the phone, he decided Anita needed to know his findings. In the next breath, he listened for her to answer his call.

"Good Hope Christian Day School." She sounded sweeter than jelly donuts. He pictured her poised at her desk, with the laughter of children in the background.

"I'm calling for information." Regan masked his voice, indicating a woman. "My children need a good school, one with structure and discipline."

"We have only a few openings. How old are your children?"

He grinned and continued the charade. "Oh, I have triplets, and they're five."

"Kindergarten age." Anita's professionalism did not waiver. "And what are their names?"

Regan covered the receiver to keep from laughing. "Larry, Curly, and Moe."

"Regan," she said softly. "You're a case."

"How did you know it was me?"

"Instinct." She laughed. "Pathetic, real pathetic."

"Did I make your day?" *I think I'd like to.*

"Absolutely, with popcorn and balloons."

Regan eased back in his chair. "I do have a legitimate reason for calling."

"This had better be good."

He took a long breath. "Seriously, Anita, I have an announcement to make in the morning, and I wanted you to know about it before you read the paper."

"And?" Her voice quivered.

"The fire the other night at Harringer's Building Supplies? Well, I have strong reasons to believe it was arson."

"Any suspects?"

"Possibly. I have to finish my investigation first."

"But your job is inspections and issuing licenses, not fire investigations."

"True, but I have a personal interest in this case, so I'm working with the fire marshal who has jurisdiction here."

Silence invaded before she spoke again. "You think Craig did it?"

You know I do. "Don't know for certain. I'm lacking something called evidence. He owns the building, and I heard from a pretty good source that his dad cut off his funds."

"Can you tell me what you found, or should I wait to read it in the morning paper?"

"It's really no secret. The wires to the burglar and fire alarm had been disconnected, plus the office had a broken window indicating point of entry."

"Be careful, Regan. I don't think Craig plays by any rules but his own."

"My thoughts exactly, but with this on his mind, he should leave you alone."

"Or make matters worse."

❧

Anita glanced to her right to see if Tyler peddled close beside her.

"I'm keeping up," he called, giving her an impish grin.

"See, I told you I would."

"I think he likes his bicycle." Regan chuckled. "Theresa knows what little boys want for their birthdays."

"And he'd outgrown his training wheels." Anita caught Regan's gaze and tossed him a smile. Somewhere in their brief journey of friendship, she'd come to feel comfortable around him. No longer did she resent his ability to say the right things or his uncanny ability to know just when to listen.

"Let's go to Grandma's," Tyler said. "Aren't we close?"

"Sure are, Sport," Regan turned to Anita and softly asked, "What do you think?"

She nodded. "Mom won't mind. She's most likely outside raking leaves or gathering pecans out of that huge tree in her yard. Although, she might put us all to work."

In less than twenty minutes, the three arrived at Mom's. As Anita had predicted, her mother was busily raking leaves, all the while ordering the ones still clinging to the trees to stay put.

"Let me finish, Theresa." Regan swung his leg over his bike. "I bet Tyler could lend a hand too."

"Sure, Grandma. Us men will have it done in no time." Anita laughed at his seriousness. *I need to hold onto every moment. He'll grow up sooner than I want.*

"Whew, you can have the job." Her mother handed Regan the rake. "Anita and I will have a little chat while you men work." She winked at Regan, and he plopped a kiss on her forehead.

Anita remembered the way Vince always felt a little peculiar around her mother. He simply didn't understand Mom's personality. She said what she thought and didn't care if you agreed or not. Daddy used to say Mom could make friends with a fence post, and on Sunday morning, she'd have 'em in church.

Regan obviously didn't have any problems with Mom. He enjoyed her. *Am I comparing Vince and Regan again? What am I doing?*

Anita refilled Regan and Tyler's water bottles and delivered them before stepping inside with her mother.

"I love hard work, but those two will have the yard looking good in half the time it takes me." Her mother sunk into a padded kitchen chair.

"You know Tyler and I would do anything for you. Please don't work so hard when we're close." Anita followed the trail of her nose, and her mouth watered. "Are you baking a pecan pie?"

Her mother nodded. "Two of them. Why don't the three of you join me for supper?"

"The three of us?" Anita laughed.

Her mother looked about, then whispered, "He's a good man, Anita."

Here comes the matchmaking. "Yes, he is Mom, and Tyler adores him."

"What about you?" Mom wiggled her shoulders.

"I adore Tyler too."

Her mother raised a brow, her round face tightening. "You know exactly what I'm talking about. How do you feel about Regan? I mean are there sparks in the air?"

Will the fireman jokes ever end? "He's a nice man, Mom, and we're good friends. I was thinking on the way over here how comfortable I feel around him."

"He'd make a good husband and father."

Anita felt her stomach turn a flip-flop. "I had a husband, and Tyler had a father—the best."

Her mother tilted her head. "You can't prosper in the future if you're dwelling in the past."

Anita stiffened in the chair, then reached to touch her ring finger, but she'd removed her wedding band months ago. "I'm doing perfectly fine in the present."

Her mother tapped her hot pink acrylic nails on the table. "You are as stubborn as I am, but I have the benefit of age and wisdom. In case you've been too blind to see what is right in front of your face, Regan Moore is quite taken with you and Tyler. Looks to me like God is trying to tell you something."

"I hadn't noticed." Anita lifted her chin.

Her mother pointed a finger in her face. "You, my dear daughter, are not too old that I can't wash your mouth out with soap for lying!"

"I believe those types of discipline are termed child abuse." Anita punctuated her reply with a nod but broke the moment with a giggle.

"Sue me, Sweetheart. I'm right as rain—and you know it."

❧

"No!" came the piercing cry through the quiet apartment.

Anita flung her magazine aside and raced to Tyler's bedroom. "I'm coming, Honey. I'm coming."

She pushed open his door. She never completely closed it for she never knew when a nightmare would occur—or the next.

"Mommy."

Only in times like these did Tyler resort to calling her this. "I'm coming." She hurried to his side and gathered him up in her arms. His little body trembled in the aftermath of his horrifying dream. "It's all right, Baby," Anita soothed. "Mommy's here. I have you."

Tyler snuggled against her, his tears wetting her T-shirt. Slowly, his rapid breathing returned to normal until he finally relaxed against her.

Such fun they'd had all day: riding his new bicycle with Regan, then pedaling to her mother's where they enjoyed a wonderful meal.

"Are you better now?" She rested her head atop his and smelled the baby shampoo used this evening.

"I think so. Mr. Regan was in it."

"Regan?" *He's never been a part of the nightmares before.*

"Yes, Mommy. We were in his Jeep, and he needed to buy

licorice. So we stopped by the gas-station store beside the soccer field. You know where that is?"

She nodded, running her fingers through his hair.

"He told me to wait while he went inside. I waited and waited. Then it got dark, and the lights went out in the store. I called for him, but he didn't come back. No one came, and I got scared, real scared. That's when I woke up." Tyler paused. "Can we call Mr. Regan? I just want to know he's okay."

Anita knew it was around ten-thirty, a little late to be calling. The last time she'd made a call at this hour, she'd woken him. "Can it wait until morning? I'm sure he's perfectly fine."

Tyler pulled from her chest. "Please. I don't want anything to happen to Mr. Regan."

His pleadings tore at her heart. Regan wouldn't mind; she felt certain. "Let me get the phone."

"I'll go with you."

Hand in hand, they ventured into the living room where her phone lay on the coffee table. She punched in the numbers to Regan's home. *Be there, Regan.* He answered on the second ring.

"Regan, this is Anita."

"What's wrong?"

She took a deep breath to calm her nerves. "I'm fine. It's Tyler. He had a bad dream, and you were in it. He wants to make sure you're all right."

"Oh, I'm sorry. Let me talk to him." The sound of his voice against the backdrop of her fears emitted strength—something she needed right now.

"Thank you." She handed the phone to Tyler and wrapped her arm around his shoulders.

He quickly recounted his nightmare. "Would you come over?"

Anita held her breath. How much could her son expect of one man? He shouldn't have to be traipsing out at this hour?

"He'll be here in a few minutes," Tyler whispered and

handed her the phone. "He hung up."

"I'm sure he will make you feel better." She understood Tyler needed to see his friend had not fallen prey to the nightmare, but what an imposition on Regan.

Slowly her thoughts focused on a new realization. The awareness both sickened and angered her, and she couldn't deny its poison. In Tyler's mind, Regan must have replaced Vince, his father. How could Regan do such a thing, play with a child's emotions until her precious son had a nightmare? He wasn't his father, not even a relative, but merely a volunteer from Big Brothers. He'd taken on Tyler as a project as repayment for her mother's compassion when his family died. Regan Moore had no business taking any position in Tyler's life other than a friend.

"Mom, are you crying?"

What is wrong with me? I can't allow Tyler to see me upset. Anita whisked away any semblance of tears. "No, Honey."

"My bad dreams will go away." He turned and laid his head on her lap. Reaching up, he touched her cheek. "Don't cry, my pretty mommy."

Unable to speak, Anita tried without success to stop the flow of liquid emotion. The tears she'd kept simmering below the surface now gushed forward.

"My Jesus will make them go away. Regan said so. Jesus is my Champion."

Anita felt the blood from her veins slam to a halt. Not only had Regan snatched up Vince's spot in Tyler's heart, but he'd also planted fantasy ideas about Jesus in his head. Matters could not grow much worse.

"I love Regan," the little boy said. "He and Jesus are my best friends."

twelve

Regan scrambled for the keys on his dresser. In his haste, he knocked them to the floor. When he bent to retrieve them, he noticed his tennis shoes weren't tied. As he quickly looped the strings into shape, his mind raced with Tyler's nightmare. How strange, nearly incredulous the boy's bad dreams now included him. What could be the source of Tyler's trauma?

Watching his father disappear in a lake of murky water is horrifying enough for a little guy. Why include me? I'm only trying to help. As he pieced together what Anita had revealed to him about her son's life, the picture slowly unfolded.

The boy didn't have a living grandfather, uncle, or any male relatives. All were gone, leaving him alone. Maybe he blamed himself, possibly feeling he'd done something to cause their demise. Perhaps he simply had an immense fear of death, anxious he might be the next. In any event, the little boy didn't have a single man in his life but Regan.

Grasping the doorknob leading from his apartment, he met with stark reality. *Tyler's afraid I'll abandon him too.*

If Regan had guessed the cause of the boy's fears, how long before Anita did the same—if not already? He knew he was a rookie psychologist at best, and some trained professional surely had to come to the same conclusion. Still, he couldn't help but wonder if any of Tyler's past therapists played an intricate part in the nightmares.

Love might be the key to unlock Tyler's troubled mind. The boy showed his affection as openly as any secure child, and Regan had responded with the same freedom. He hadn't really pondered the matter before, yet he cared for the boy. Tyler had drawn him into his world with an impish grin and a gentle spirit. *I'm going to ask Anita how she feels about having him talk about his dad—the good things he remembers.*

Regan glanced at his hand still circling the doorknob. If he admitted the truth, Anita had captured a big chunk of his heart too. He dared not say a word, not until she worked out her relationship with the Lord. Her eyes held such pain, a deep longing, but she'd have to make the discovery that God wanted to heal her brokenness.

Within fifteen minutes, Regan was climbing the steps to Anita's apartment. He had no clue what to say to Tyler other than to listen and assure him dreams were not reality. Regan and Tyler had prayed together in the past, although Anita would most likely protest.

With a heavy sigh, he rang the doorbell. Never, absolutely never, did he consider volunteering for Big Brothers would cause such emotional turmoil.

"Hey," he said, neither offering nor forcing a smile.

The amber streaks in her pale blue eyes flashed like lightning. "Thanks for coming." She stepped away from the door, much farther than necessary.

"Has Tyler gone back to sleep?"

Anita shook her head. Silence invaded the moment as a cold glance spoke fathoms of her unsettled emotions. "He's playing a computer game; I'll tell him you're here."

She whirled around to fetch the boy. Regan stopped her. "Can we talk afterwards, if it's not too late?"

"I suppose. What about?" Her glacier tone left no doubt to her irritability about something.

"Tyler, and why I might have been the focus of his nightmare tonight."

Her hardened gaze bore straight into his. "I have reached a few conclusions myself."

"All right." *What have I done, unless she has reached the same conclusion as I have?* Forcing a smile, he headed down the hall to the boy's room.

Alone with Tyler, Regan tucked him into bed and sat cross-legged on the floor beside him. "Sorry about your bad dream, Sport."

"I have them a lot." Tyler stared up at the ceiling where a fan whirled on slow speed.

The only sound came from a distant police siren.

"Are they always the same?"

"No, Sir, but until tonight they were always about my dad. Sometimes I forget what he looked like. Then I look at his picture on my dresser."

Regan stared up at the photo, although he'd seen it before. It was the three of them standing on a pier and holding up a string of big-mouth bass. Vince's arms wrapped around Anita and Tyler on either side of him. Regan wished he'd known the man; he looked like a great guy.

"You and your mom look real happy."

Tyler's eyes pooled, and he hastily blinked them back.

Regan touched his arm. "Don't be afraid to cry. A real man is not afraid of tears."

His gaze met Regan's. "Mom says that too, but she almost never cries—well, she did tonight."

Regan needed to explore Anita's reaction, but how far dared he go? "You have a wonderful mom, Sport. Did she cry because you had the bad dream?"

Tyler glanced up at the ceiling again, and Regan waited. "Mostly when I told her not to cry."

Regan pressed his lips together in an effort to form a faint smile. "She loves you."

He nodded. "I know, and I told her I loved you and Jesus."

Bingo. That's what he'd seen in Anita's eyes, not just anger, but fear. . .fear of losing Tyler.

"I told her what you said about Jesus being the best in every sport, and He'd help me with soccer even if we didn't win and He'd help me with the other stuff I do." In the faint light of his lamp, Tyler's face glowed. He knew Jesus.

The innocence of a child, Lord. If we all could embrace You with the same trust.

"Sport, I love you too." A lump rested in Regan's throat. For the first time, he had a glimpse of what Anita felt for her son. He understood her protective nature.

"Thanks. I'm glad you came. I was feeling awful about the dream. I talked to Jesus about it when I was 'posed to be playing on Mom's computer. Can we pray for Jesus to take away the bad dreams?"

"That sounds like a good idea."

Tyler pulled his hands from beneath the blanket and folded them while Regan prayed. "Dear Jesus, we're asking you to take away Tyler's bad dreams. He wants to sleep every night without being afraid another one might happen. Only You can do this. Give him peaceful rest all the time." Regan peered at the boy clenching his eyes shut. "Would you like to say something to Jesus?"

Tyler nodded. "Jesus, I love You like Regan and my Sunday school teacher and Pastor Miller say. Last week I asked You to live in my heart, remember? Now, I'm wonderin' if You'll take away my awful dreams. Thank You for being my friend."

Out of the mouths of children. "In Jesus' name, amen."

Within fifteen minutes, Tyler once more slept. Regan snapped off the lamp and exited the room, being careful not to shut the door completely as Anita preferred. He had no intention of angering her, especially when he sensed a lengthy conversation in the offing. Determined to speak his mind, he took resolute steps in her direction.

Anita sat on the living-room sofa, staring into the silent darkness. She turned to view him, her pale face emitting a sorrow much too deep for anyone to bear.

"He's asleep," Regan said.

She lifted her chin in acknowledgment. "Do you still want to talk?"

"Yes, if you're not too tired."

She folded her hands in her lap, as though ready for an interrogation.

Are you going to shut me out? He moved toward the lamp and switched it on before sitting on the opposite end of the sofa. "Has Tyler ever had nightmares before about someone other than his father?"

"No."

"Has he ever formed an attachment with any therapists?"

"No." She crossed her arms.

"Anita, what's wrong? I've talked to Tyler, and I'm sure he said some things to you that were upsetting."

For the first time he gained eye contact. "I admit I'm disturbed about some of it."

Lord, help me. "Are you going to explain? Then again, I think I can guess."

"Be my guest."

His palms grew sweaty. "There are three things rolling around in my head: one, his nightmare included me; two, he told you he loved me; and three, he talked about his relationship with Jesus."

Her lips quivered, and she stiffened. "You're very observant."

Regan leaned closer to her. "Don't you think I love that kid? He's the best there is, Anita. I'm honored he cares for me." She continued to stare at him, as though her emotions had been bound into some strangling hold. "I haven't stolen him from you. . .or Vince. I've simply shown him we all have room in our hearts to love more people."

She started to speak, then hesitated. He sat back and watched her, begging for her to see he meant no harm. "What about religion? I don't want my son making a decision about Christianity until he's older and can make a wise choice."

He wanted to scream at her; she had once experienced an intimate relationship with the Lord. She was wrong to deny Tyler. "I can't stop telling Tyler about Jesus Christ any more than I can stop breathing."

"Even if it means you can't see him anymore?"

Anger wound its way around his heart. Anita had insulted his Lord, and he refused to allow it. "If you want to take out your bitterness toward God on me, that's your business, but don't degrade God and expect me to say nothing—"

"You have no right to persuade my son toward your beliefs." Her voice hardened.

"I have every right."

He stood from the sofa, so enraged he could not stay a minute longer. "Go ahead and bar me from seeing Tyler if it makes you feel better. Keep him in your little cocoon and see what good it does. He won't always be a child, and one day your smothering will drive him away." He stopped in an effort to squelch his temper. "Let me tell you this. Your decision is not in his best interests, but yours." In three strides, he opened the apartment door and left before he said a whole lot more.

Anita had pushed his limits. Jealousy's slimy green tentacles were strangling the life out of her and forcing Tyler to grow into a fearful, mentally and spiritually ill, young man. No wonder he had nightmares. How would that child ever grow up to love and act responsibly when his own mother rejected God's principles? Both were headed for disaster. The thought gave a whole new meaning to dysfunctional.

Once Regan had disarmed his Jeep, his rash words jolted his brain. *What makes me think I have all the answers? She needs understanding not condemnation.*

Regan rammed his fist into his palm. His self-righteous piety made him want to gag. Some role model he turned out to be.

❧

Anita sat stunned on the sofa. She balled her fists, desperately trying to ward off the fury threatening to explode. She'd given in to tears tonight against her better judgment. Now anger pounded on her heart's door. Control. She must master control. Weeping buckets solved nothing; temper tantrums displayed an animal mentality. Struggle through life and let no one in. Only Tyler mattered. He gave her a reason to open her eyes in the morning when she'd rather roll over and die.

She caught her breath. She'd run Regan off. However would she explain his absence to Tyler? Her mind spun. Lying didn't suit her. Telling the truth might turn him against her. She knew best, didn't she? Mothers always recognized danger for their children. He'd get over it.

Would she?

God. Jesus. Vince. Tyler. Regan. What were the answers plaguing her life? For that matter, she didn't know the questions.

A light knock on the door startled her, and although she felt a twinge of alarm at the lateness of the hour, she welcomed the diversion from her pounding thoughts.

Rising to her shaking legs, Anita stumbled to the door and peered through the security peephole. Regan. Hadn't he done enough damage for one night?

"I don't want to talk to you," she said barely above a whisper.

Another knock.

Surely he hadn't heard her, but if she talked any louder, Tyler would waken. Her only choice lay in confronting him on the opposite side of the door. Releasing the dead bolt, she jerked the door open. "What do you want?" She avoided his gaze.

"To apologize for losing my temper."

Her tremulous emotions flowed through her body like waves crashing against the shore. *I wish you'd just leave me alone.*

"I said some things I shouldn't have."

Anita focused her attention on the light post behind him. "Did you mean them?"

He sighed. "I was angry. I never wanted or tried to take Tyler away from you."

He's all I have. Don't you understand? She found the courage to peer into his eyes. Even in the dark, she knew the steely blue gaze that so often radiated warmth and kindness was still there.

"I know life and all its pressures are hard for you," he continued. "My commitment to Tyler was to possibly help rid him of the nightmares, nothing more."

She didn't know what to say. How much easier for her to respond if he were angry. She felt drained, her very lifeblood slowly trickling away.

"I'm so tired." She wrapped her arms around her chest. "Seems like I'm fighting an army I can't see. Life keeps getting harder." She tore away from his gaze. "I'm. . .I'm sorry too. You are so good for Tyler, and he loves you. How awful of me to consider breaking the bond between you." Her throat tightened. The aching sobs building inside begged to be released. She trembled uncontrollably and willed the heaviness in her chest to lighten. "I'm so tired of fighting alone, Regan."

He reached for her, and she fell limp into his arms. The floodgates of sorrow and despair unleashed against his chest. She couldn't stop the flow. Surely she'd drown in her own sea of misery.

Time ceased its meaning and purpose as she wept. Loneliness beginning the day Vince died coursed through her body and whirled her into a vortex of grief. The fierce love she possessed for Tyler and the fear of losing him gripped her heart. She didn't want to feel this pain, and yet it continued to surface until she no longer had a tear left to shed.

I'm such a weakling. Anita lifted her head from his chest. "I don't know what to say." He stroked her hair, or perhaps he'd been doing it all the while she cried.

"You don't have to say anything. Tears are healing, you know."

"Did they help you?" she whispered, grateful for the dim

light of the doorway.

"Oh, yes. The Bible tells us there's a time for grieving."

"I remember." For once the mention of the Bible didn't anger her. She remembered a time when the Psalms eased every care from her mind, when every word filled her with love and awe for the Almighty God. Sometimes she wanted to go back there again. Pulling back from him, Anita rubbed her arms. She needed a tissue. "Your shirt's soaked."

"I don't mind."

"I. . .I need to go inside now." *I'm so embarrassed.*

He brushed a stray tear from her wet cheeks. "Will you be okay?"

She nodded.

Regan lifted her chin. "Don't give up on me."

Startled at the very words she'd been thinking about herself, she stared up into his chiseled face. The lamplight behind him cast a bit of a halo around his head, not ethereal by any means, but it made him appear strong, and she desperately craved strength. "We're so very different, you and I." With those words, she stepped back inside her apartment and shut the door.

Tomorrow she'd deal with the fool she'd made of herself tonight. Tomorrow she'd have logic and a clear mind to help make the right decisions about Tyler. . .about herself. . .about Regan. . .and about God, who seemed to be calling from the depths of her very soul.

thirteen

Anita stared at the antique trunk in the living room. She'd thought about its contents all day at work, and now that Tyler had fallen asleep, the urge to sort through the contents plagued her again. With her arms hanging limply at her side, she stood over it. *Do I honestly want to torment myself with what's inside?* Slowly she eased to the floor, debating, fighting, yet feeling compelled to open the trunk—for inside was her Bible.

She wanted the joy of walking with the Lord again, but she hadn't gotten over her anger yet. One voice invited her to bask in His love. A darker voice whispered a rededication to God promised an abusive relationship with Him—she'd be hurt time and time again. God didn't really care.

In her heart she knew differently. She well remembered His promises and the joy of allowing God to lead her life. The past few weeks had knocked the wind out of her. She needed the very thing she feared the most.

Anita lifted the leather strap and released the trunk lid, but she still couldn't bring herself to lift the lid. After last night's humiliating display of temper and tears, she realized something in her life had to change. Her emotions were out of control. Everything had become unmanageable: her position at Good Hope, her relationship with her son, Regan's commitment to Tyler, her mother's insistent demands to participate in church functions, Craig Harringer's threats.

The inability to handle day-to-day stress frightened her. How well Anita remembered her first panic attack right after Vince had died. The symptoms sent alarming sensations through her body—racing heartbeat, terror, nausea, difficulty in breathing, and a foreboding about death. Last night she'd feared the old sensations would creep back into her life. Tonight she vowed to do whatever was needed to put her life in order, but courage failed her.

Could God be the answer? Did He really want her to return to Him? So many questions and no answers. How could she ever accept Vince's death had been a part of God's divine plan?

Her hands grasped the trunk lid and lifted. Inside, near the bottom of the stacks of sympathy cards, newspaper clippings, and letters of condolence, rested the Bible her parents had presented to Vince and her on their wedding day. Their name and wedding date had been engraved in gold at the bottom right hand corner of the dark green leather binding. Vince and Anita had been faithful to Bible study and prayer all of their married lives. She'd stopped the day of his accident.

Her fingers brushed across the grainy cover, and she recalled the many times Vince had opened its pages and read aloud. Closing her eyes, she could almost hear his voice, the words spoken in reverence and love. He began reading passages to their unborn child and continued after Tyler's birth.

Anita leafed through the Bible until she came to Isaiah. This was one of Vince's favorite books. The pages were full of his notes in the margins, and many underlined verses in various colors of ink revealed how the words had spoken to him at different times. Her gaze fell on chapter 61.

Before they were married, Vince had memorized this passage. He'd been a victim of child abuse at the hands of alcoholic parents, and he'd spent many years in and out of foster homes. During this time of his life, he found the Lord while living with a Christian family. Isaiah 61 helped him to love his birth parents and encourage them to seek medical help. Vince had beaten the odds to live a healthy and productive life through Jesus Christ.

Anita had forgotten this aspect of Vince's life until now.

He never doubted God or the power of His Word. No matter what happened to him, Vince always claimed the Creator's love and unfailing promises. She could almost hear him. . . Anita sucked in a breath. Vince wouldn't have wanted her to hold onto this bitterness. For that matter, neither did God.

Oh, Heavenly Father, I don't want to deny You, but there's so much I don't understand. I used to believe Your love surpassed all boundaries, but now my heart feels as if it's been shattered into irreparable pieces. Nothing I do eases the pain. I really need peace and reassurance. I'm afraid of losing Tyler, being alone, and countless other things that seem to haunt me day and night.

Lowering her gaze to the page, she began to read chapter 61, her attention focused on words in the first verse: "He has sent me to bind up the brokenhearted, to proclaim freedom for the captives and release from the darkness for the prisoners."

A sob escaped her throat, and she hastily blinked back the tears. Her prayer had barely been uttered and already God had answered. On she read: "To provide for those who grieve in Zion—to bestow on them a crown of beauty instead of ashes, the oil of gladness instead of mourning, and a garment of praise instead of a spirit of despair."

Anita clung to each word, as though the Lord Jesus sat beside her on the floor and held her hand as He spoke: "They will rebuild the ancient ruins and restore the places long devastated; they will renew the ancient cities."

"Oh, Lord. Can you rebuild this ruin? Can you restore me to the woman I once was?" Her mother's words echoed around the room. *Honey, when we don't understand what God is doing in our lives, we have to trust His unfailing love.*

She had no choice but to put her faith and trust back into the Father God who offered her His perfect love. She hated not knowing why Vince died, and hated it even more that she might never learn why, but her questions must go unanswered. *My ways are not your ways.* Someday she could ask

God why He took Vince from her and the son who needed him, but for now all of Anita's ways of reclaiming joy and purpose in her life had failed. She needed God to guide her. Cradling her face in her hands, she prayed for forgiveness and asked Him to heal her broken heart.

❧

Regan couldn't get Anita off his mind. Yesterday, he'd wanted to call her, but a nudging at his mind stopped him each time he reached for the phone. Saturday, Tyler had a scheduled soccer game, one in which the boys would travel to a nearby town. Regan wanted to ask Anita and Tyler to ride with him, but in light of Tuesday night he hesitated.

Taking a quick glimpse at his watch, Regan saw the hour had arrived to meet with deputy fire investigator David Steiner, assigned to arson cases in the area. A knock at his office door confirmed the matter. Within five minutes, David, a tall stern-faced man, finished with pleasantries and channeled the conversation toward the warehouse fire.

"Forced entry." David kept his attention on the investigation report. His bushy eyebrows narrowed. "What has the owner said? Did he indicate any enemies?"

"He called yesterday and offered complete cooperation."

"Any reason to believe he might be a suspect?" David asked.

"A few." Regan pulled out a list he'd started on Craig. "Let me run through this, and you can tell me what you think."

Once Regan finished reading, David made a few notes. The smell of stale tobacco odors surrounded the investigator. "A hothead who needs money, huh?"

"I'd like to nail him."

"Sounds personal."

"It is. Fire's always personal, and he threatened a good friend of mine and her son."

"Ordinarily I'd say stick to the indicators, except his past pushes my suspicions to the top," David said. "Let's head to the warehouse. I'm ready to proceed with the investigation."

At the site, David and Regan walked the perimeters and searched through all the areas destroyed by the fire. They found nothing.

"I want to see the area of forced entry," David announced. "Like you, I don't understand why the burglar alarm didn't go off as soon as someone entered the office, unless our fire-bug had a key and already knew the code."

"You know my thoughts on the matter," Regan said. This part of the warehouse received minimal damage, and he believed that aspect would be to the investigator's advantage.

David flipped on his camcorder, aiming the camera on the broken glass where the arsonist supposedly climbed through the office window from outside the building. "Nothing looks out of the ordinary here. The glass is basically on the inside of the office. Regan, let's follow the path from the window to the closet door where our man disconnected the wires to the burglar and fire alarm systems."

Clearly, the knob and lock had been pried open. "The markings on the crowbar match those on the door knob and lock," Regan said.

David studied the door. "Once the window had been shattered, the burglar alarm should have gone off."

An idea tugged at Regan's mind. "I have an idea."

The camera followed him to the closet where he examined the damaged door and lock. He opened it slowly, remembering a peculiar impression on the inside knob. His suspicions were correct. "The knob on the inside has the indentation of one blow, as though the arsonist was nervous. I'm thinking he hit this without thinking."

David turned off the camcorder. "Now I'm thinking like you. Do you suppose this is an inside job? Our man could have unlocked the front door, stepped inside to the closet, unlocked it, disconnected the wires, then made the closet look like forced entry. He meant to tamper with the outer knob but accidentally hit the inner one. Once he made the closet look like forced entry, he set the fire in the warehouse, walked back to the front office, locked up, then broke the glass. That would answer why the burglar alarm never went off."

"Guess we can ask Harringer a few questions—like who else has a key. If he didn't set the fire, my bet is he knows who did. After all, he offered his full cooperation."

ঌ

Anita held her breath while she waited for her mother to answer the phone. "Mom?" This conversation would be tough. She'd never been one who easily confessed to wrongdoing.

"Hi, Honey. You doing okay? Sound a bit tired."

"I'm fine, but I do have something to tell you."

"Has that Harringer been harassing you or Tyler again? Because if he is, I'm heading to the police department and—"

"Hold it, Mom. This is nothing bad. In fact, you'll be very pleased."

"Is it about you and Regan?"

Anita laughed despite her nervousness. She took a sip of her diet cola, letting the cool bubbles momentarily distract her. "No, this is better." When her mother didn't reply, Anita ventured forward. "I made a rededication to Jesus Christ."

She heard the sobs. "I'm so happy for you."

"I know you are, and I really appreciate the many times you've prayed for me. I've been horrible, and I know it."

"You were simply walking through the wilderness. Have you told Tyler?"

"Yes, I told him this morning before dropping him off at school. My sweet little boy said he'd prayed for Jesus to live in his heart too—and asked Him to take away his nightmares."

"I bet he was so excited. We've prayed together about you."

"I figured as much. In fact he said so. Today was the first time the two of us have prayed together since Vince died. I don't want to ever lose that closeness to my son again."

She heard her mom sniff. "What about Regan?"

"That's another reason why I called. Would you mind if

I'm a few minutes late picking up Tyler this afternoon? I wanted to run by Regan's office after school."

"Do I mind? Does the sun come up in the east? The only reason why Tyler doesn't live here is because his mother believes in independence."

"Great, Mom. Thanks. I love you." Hanging up the phone, she noted a serious churning in the pit of her stomach. Getting sick was not on her list of accomplishments for the day. She simply needed to tell Regan about her spiritual renewal and apologize for past mistakes—a whole bunch of them.

After school, Anita drove by the fire marshal's office. She didn't know whether to pray he wouldn't be there or hope his easygoing manner helped tell him she'd renewed her faith. Sitting in her car and thinking about the rehearsed speech only caused her heart to pound harder. With a sigh, she realized she couldn't wait forever. Snatching up her purse, she headed toward the one-story brick building.

Anita hadn't been to the fire marshal's office before, and a bit of familiarity would have helped ground her trembling legs. She stepped into Regan's office and waited while his secretary, an older woman with a kindly smile, phoned him.

"Mrs. Todd." She replaced the receiver. "Mr. Moore is in a meeting, but it's about to conclude if you'd like to wait."

The fluttering against her chest mounted, and she feared the secretary might hear. "I can. . .for a little while." Picking up a book about single parenting she'd found in the church library during her lunch break, Anita elected to read, or rather try to. She quickly found out her comprehension level was a fraction above zero.

Just when she'd decided to write a note and leave, the office door opened, and two men walked out with Regan. Craig Harringer looked none too pleased.

"I want you to get to the bottom of this." He shook his finger at Regan and the other man. "Torched! I won't have it. This fire has already put me into financial ruin, and now I earn someone set it." He whirled around and saw Anita. "There's your first suspect. She's had it in for me since the day I tried to politely pick up my daughter from school."

Pure rage emitted from Anita's flesh. With all the things this man had done, how dare he accuse her of anything as demeaning as arson? *Calm down. God is right here with you. He knows the unfairness here.* She toyed with the idea of responding or simply ignoring him and his nasty accusation.

"So where were you the night of the fire?" Craig's voice mounted with each word.

"Harringer." Regan's voice rang sharp and forceful.

Anita held up her hand in defense. "I have an alibi. But since you are so quick to accuse, where were you?"

Craig clenched his fists. "I was having dinner with my parents." He stepped closer. "I know what you've done, Miss Lily White Church Lady, and I intend to prove it."

fourteen

Regan felt his blood rush hot to his face. It took all his strength to keep from telling Craig exactly what he thought of his bullying techniques. "At this point, we will conduct the investigation and question any valid suspects, not you. I believe the police report at the preschool entailed a few more factors than what you just stated."

Craig shrugged. "Whatever. But I'm telling you, that Todd woman is out to get me. She's probably working with my ex-wife to discredit my fine family name."

No, Craig, you've done an excellent job of that all by yourself.

"We appreciate your cooperation," David said. "We'll be in touch as we work through the investigative process."

"Make it soon. I have paying customers who need a place to store what's left of their building supplies." He turned to Anita. "You will be hearing from my attorney. In fact, all of you will. I believe my fire is part of a conspiracy." Craig stomped out of the office.

Silence lingered for a moment.

"I'm sorry, Anita." Regan hoped his words conveyed the sincerity he felt.

She offered a faint smile. "I'm considering the source."

He nodded, noting a change in her but not quite sure what he actually saw. "Anita, this is David Steiner, the deputy fire investigator assigned to our district."

She stood up and extended her hand. "It's a pleasure to meet you, Mr. Steiner. I'm Anita Todd."

Why have I not noticed how lovely you are?

"Regan told me about the unfortunate circumstances with

Mr. Harringer and your school. Believe me, his accusations are simply unwarranted."

"Thank you." She turned to Regan. "I didn't mean to interrupt anything here. I can visit with you later."

"Absolutely not," David said. "I'm leaving. Got lots of work to do, which will keep me busy for hours."

"Dinner at six-thirty?" Regan asked.

David nodded. "Pleasure to meet you, Mrs. Todd." He left the office, leaving Regan alone with Anita and his secretary.

"This can wait." Anita tucked her book inside the top opening of her purse.

"And deny me the company of a beautiful lady?" Despite their past differences, he meant every word. He ushered her inside and closed the door, watching as she nervously sat across from his cluttered desk.

He immediately went to work assembling the notes and reports about the Harringer fire into one pile.

"Regan," she said with a light laugh, "I didn't come here to see your desk."

He glanced up and once again noted the softness in her eyes. . .something had changed. *Is this a move in a positive direction?* "Great, but I want you to know I'm not always this disorganized." Flashes of their first meeting skipped across his mind.

"I know. I only want to tell you something."

He eased into his chair. "Go ahead. You have my complete attention."

She hesitated. "I've been doing some soul searching. I don't have all the answers, but I made enough observations to understand how wrong I've been."

"About what?"

"Life, my son, you, but mostly God."

"And?"

"Last night I made a rededication to Jesus Christ."

He couldn't stop the smile spreading across his face.

"Wonderful. I knew I saw something different in your eyes." His heart slammed against his chest. He wanted to holler like a school kid. "I bet Theresa is excited."

Her gaze reflected the smile tugging at the corners of her mouth. "Oh yeah. She's planning this huge Italian dinner tonight."

"I wonder if that has anything to do with a phone call inviting me to dinner?"

"Could be."

"Does she make Italian wedding cake too?"

She wrinkled her nose at him. "Absolutely. Melts in your mouth." Her facial expression changed to serious. "I also need to say I'm sorry for the many times I've been rude."

He chuckled. "I believe I head the top of the list in that department."

"You had one bad day—I've had a couple of bad years." She tugged at her ear, twirling the pearl earring decorating it. "Guess I said all I intended. Will you continue to work with Tyler?"

"Of course. Would you consider letting me drive to the game on Saturday?"

"If I can buy lunch for the three of us." Anita ceased toying with the earring and combed her fingers through her hair. She stood and hoisted her purse onto her shoulder. "So I'll see you later?"

He shook his head. "I'm supposed to have dinner with David, but you could save me a piece of cake."

"I will." She glanced down at the carpeted floor then back up at him. "How long do you think the investigation will take?"

"Hard to say. We've decided, at least at this point, to keep the public informed of our findings."

She tilted her head. "You know it frightens me because I'm afraid Craig had a hand in it."

He didn't know how to respond. He wanted to protect her,

tell her he and David would learn the truth, but she'd already seen Craig in action. Frankly, Regan didn't trust the man any farther than he could throw him. "I'm doing my best, and I'm praying through every step of the way."

"I. . .will pray for you too."

"Thanks. Can I give you a hug?"

She nodded. Her hair fell about her shoulders in soft dark waves. Her blue eyes streaked with gold reminded him of a burst of sunshine across a clear sky. A hug was a beginning, and how he yearned for more than friendship.

❧

"We simply have a good friendship," Anita said to Susan the following day.

"Right. That's why he sent you a dozen red roses?"

Anita pretended annoyance and leaned over to take in the delectable scent of the roses. "He's simply pleased I've made a rededication to the Lord," she whispered, so none of the staff would hear she hadn't been exactly what they assumed in Christian leadership.

"I'm tickled too, and I've prayed ever since you moved back to Sweetwell, but I didn't send flowers."

"He is helping Tyler," Anita pointed out, avoiding her friend while straightening her desk.

"Darlin'," Susan said, exaggerating her southern drawl, "what did the card say?"

The phone rang, saving Anita from the embarrassment of reading Susan the card. Unfortunately, her friend waited beside her desk until Anita finished the call.

"One of the moms is concerned about her son's social skills." Anita replaced the phone. "She wants a conference in the morning."

"How old is he?"

"Four, and he really is a bright child. She says her husband is upset because he prefers books and games to sports. Thinks he is introverted and will never be a football player like his dad."

"Oh, brother. Sounds like his dad has the problem."

"Exactly."

Susan rubbed her palms together. "You're not off the hook, Girlfriend. What did Regan's card say?"

Anita moaned. "You are relentless." She pulled the small envelope from the plastic spike inserted in the vase and opened it.

Susan leaned over her shoulder. "Congratulations on your decision," she read. "I know this is only the beginning. Love, Regan." She patted Anita's shoulder. "How sweet. I know he means your spiritual decision, but the next line has to be about the two of you."

I thought about the same thing—but no, he's not interested. "Friends, just friends," Anita said. "Besides, your break is up, and children are missing you. Are they memorizing their poem for the Fall Festival?"

Laughing, Susan headed toward the hallway. "Romeo, oh Romeo, wherefore art thou my Romeo?"

🐚

"I announced our findings to the *Sweetwell Tribune* this morning," Regan said. "Let's see if our man squirms."

David pulled a stick of gum from his pants' pocket. "Do you believe his story about losing a set of keys?"

"Hardly. I did a little more investigation and found out his legal debt is astronomical."

David bit into the piece of gum and tossed the wrapping in the trash. "And this is to obtain visitation rights for his daughter and the charges for the damage done to the preschool?"

Regan nodded. He liked David, but the smoke permeating from the man's clothes made Regan want to drag out a hose. "His first hearing is in a month. I sure would like to get his dad's take on the whole picture."

"Have you tried?"

"Oh, yes. He's tighter than a drum, but I did find out he

had an encouraging conversation with Craig's ex-wife. Her lawyer and I have swapped a little information. He has the same sentiments I do about the guy."

"Hmm. I really would like enough evidence to press arson charges. What about a secretary at the warehouse site?"

Regan drummed his pen on his desk. "Couldn't get a word out of her. She's jumpy as a scared cat."

"Then let's ask Mr. Cooperative if we can question her."

All the way to Craig's temporary office site, Regan hoped his hunch about the man was not motivated by vengeance. He despised the man for being the cause of the look on Anita's face when she saw Craig the day before. And when Craig had accused her of setting the fire, Regan had wanted to lay a fist up alongside his perfectly tanned jaw. Not exactly an act of Christian kindness, but he enjoyed the thought. At least he had Anita and Tyler all to himself tomorrow. He didn't worry about them when they were within his reach.

A sad realization crossed his mind. Poor Rhonda. She had no one when the despair of single parenting and Craig's abuse troubled her—no one except God. Regan knew from experience the heavenly Father met all of His children's needs. Perhaps, now that Anita had made peace with Him, she'd keep closer contact with Rhonda.

Here I am, being the caretaker again. In some counseling sessions, I would be labeled the one in need of therapy. In truth, Regan cared for people and wanted them free from hurt. Sometimes he was misunderstood and had to take a step back—another one of his faults. Regan inwardly chuckled. What he needed right now was God's direction with Anita Todd and a certain seven year old.

At the warehouse's temporary office, Craig's secretary, Alma Knight, answered their questions with her boss present. She looked none too happy about the questioning.

"Mr. Harringer stated the keys to the office were stolen.

When did this occur?" David asked, positioning a hand-held recorder.

The middle-aged woman stiffened. "About a month ago."

"Did you report them missing to the police?"

She swallowed. "No."

"Were the locks changed?"

"No." She folded her hands in her lap.

"Why not?" David persisted.

"Craig thought having another set made would be sufficient."

"Did you take care of having that done?"

"Yes."

"Where were they made?" David stared into her face, which by now had turned a shade between white and gray.

"At the hardware store."

"The one near the square?" Regan asked.

"Yes."

"Do you have a receipt?" David asked.

"I believe I lost it in the fire."

"How's that when the office received little damage?"

"Well, it's missing in my. . .my petty cash envelope."

David continued firing the inquiries. "How many people have keys?"

"Craig, his father, and myself."

"One last question, Ms. Knight," David said politely. "Where were you on the night of the fire?"

Indignation swept across the woman's face. "Mr. Steiner," she punctuated, "I was at home with my husband entertaining dinner guests—two other couples to be exact." She stiffened. "Would you like to know what was on the menu?"

"No, thank you." David smiled. "You've been most helpful, Mrs. Knight, and I appreciate it."

Alma said nothing but cast him a seething look.

Later Regan and David stopped by the hardware store. They neither remembered Alma or Craig having duplicate keys made nor had a record of the transaction.

"We've got to search deeper for the evidence," Regan said, clearly frustrated. "The way it looks now, Craig, Jacob, and Alma are all suspects."

"I wonder what our man has on his secretary that she's covering up for him?" David questioned. "There's got to be a way to find out."

fifteen

Anita sighed as Tyler gobbled the last of his French fries. "Slow down. You'll be sick."

"Yes, Ma'am." He proceeded to quickly unwrap his burger. "I'm just real hungry. Winning games does that to a man."

"The food will do its job much better if you slow down to enjoy it. Take a breather before you dive into your sandwich."

"Oh, Mom—"

She raised a brow.

"Yes, Ma'am."

Regan tossed Anita a wry grin while Tyler toyed with the paper around his burger. One of the other boys shouted at Tyler to join him on the outside playground.

"Go ahead," she said. "You can finish eating when you're done playing."

"Thanks." A moment later, Tyler disappeared into a maze of bright orange tunnels.

"You're a great mom," Regan said.

"I appreciate that. The job's not easy." She started to capture his gaze but thought better of it. An uneasiness swept over her, as though being alone with him invited trouble. . .or something.

"You're blushing," he said with one of his familiar chuckles.

Great, and I don't even know why. "No, I'm not. It's your imagination."

His hearty laugh drew the attention of those sitting around them.

"Would you hush?" she whispered. "Everyone is looking at us."

"Sure, but you're redder than ever."

This time she gathered enough courage to gaze straight into his eyes. "I'll get even, you know."

"I dare you."

Am I falling for you? I can't be. I don't want to be.

"Okay, Miss No Comment, I do have a favor to ask." Before she could say a word he continued. "I wondered if Tyler had ever been to the Arbuckle Wilderness."

Good, an easier topic. "No, but Mom has mentioned it a few times."

He took a drink of his iced tea, then slowly set it on the table. "How do you feel about driving there a week from tomorrow after church? Theresa too, if she'd like to join us."

"I believe Mom has a luncheon planned and wouldn't be available. But I suppose Tyler and I could go."

He grinned. "Then am I forgiven for teasing you?"

"Forgiven, maybe, but when you least expect it, I'll find a way to trip you up." Anita found herself laughing; she hadn't felt like this in a very long time. "I haven't been to the Arbuckles in years."

"Me, either, but I do remember the fun of driving through the reserve and feeding those animals. I'd suggest this weekend, but with Labor Day, it will be packed."

"So after church we change and head toward the great safari?" Anita asked.

"Sounds good, and let's grab lunch on the way."

"Wonderful. Tyler will love it."

❧

Sunday morning services were more beautiful than Anita ever remembered. The choir sang sweeter, the congregational hymns and choruses touched her heart with messages she needed to hear, and the sermon focused on abandoning bitterness. True worship.

Thank You for being faithful to me when I abandoned You. I need help, Lord, every minute of the day. Please remember Rhonda in her struggles with Craig, and heal Tyler of his nightmares. Amen. And Lord, are You trying to tell me something about Regan? Because I don't understand my reactions to him.

The drive down to the Chickasaw National Recreation Area in the Arbuckle Mountains proved glorious. A few of the leaves were already beginning to change, and temperatures hovered in the seventies, not unbearably hot. She found it hard to believe fall would arrive soon, ushering the promise of winter, but for today Anita intended to soak up any extra sun and enjoy the wildlife. Tyler was so excited. He'd made a mental list of all the animals he hoped to see and shared it with his mom and Regan.

Regan purchased three plastic buckets of a high protein feed mix before they set out on their six-and-a half-mile driving tour. "Tyler, some of these birds and animals will stick their heads inside the window as far as they can, especially the emus and ostriches. They have no manners when it comes to their stomachs. Keep your window partially rolled up, and listen to your Mom."

"Yes, Sir," he replied, with his usual toothless grin, although his permanent teeth were beginning to appear.

"I'll be taking lots of pictures. If we get back in time tonight, I'll download them so you can take a few prints to school."

"Awesome. I'll be real good and do what you and Mom say." His excitement grew higher as he pointed at the animals in the near distance. "What about the real wild animals?"

Amused, Anita answered him as seriously as he'd posed the question. "I believe you mean the dangerous kinds. Those are kept behind fences and cages, but you'll see them just fine from your window."

The car wound around a trail leading to a part of the reserve where a group of white-tailed deer eagerly awaited the Jeep. Moose came into view next, and while Regan drove on, camels plodded by.

"They look like they're chewing a big wad of gum," Tyler observed, "but I don't see the lions." Tyler craned his neck to look down into the thick undergrowth surrounded by tall fencing.

Anita studied the valley until she spotted a female watching them as intently as they looked for her. "There, Tyler." She pointed. The lioness's tan coat blended in well with the foliage and the first hints of fall.

"Wow," the little boy said. "Look at that, Mr. Regan. She doesn't look so mean; I bet I could pet her."

He chuckled. "Not today, Sport."

They stopped to peer into a cage where a black leopard paced back and forth as though looking to escape through the metal bars. Anita shuddered, glad the cat found residence inside the cage rather than outside.

On they drove, with ostriches and emus outnumbering any of their other following. They saw two buffalos and a rhino, but those animals were kept at a distance. The zebras caught Anita's eye. Their magnificent stance definitely belonged in the wilds of Africa, and when they ran, she expected giraffes and elephants to trail alongside them.

"Isn't this the best fun?" Tyler said. "We look like a real family."

His words yanked at her heartstrings. She knew he meant well, but was the facade of a family filling him with false illusions?

"How about the petting zoo when we're finished here?" Regan asked, breaking the uncomfortable silence. "Then I think we'll have enough time for a few rides in the amusement park."

"Cool. Wait till I tell the kids at school about this—and show them the pictures."

While Tyler lingered in the petting zoo, completely absorbed in the baby deer, baby pot-bellied pigs, a few sheep, goats, and even a baby zebra, Regan and Anita stopped to chat.

"This day has been wonderful," Anita said, as a playful sheep gave Tyler's rear a boost, and Regan snapped a picture.

"Sure has. Do you think we wore him out?"

"Maybe not him but definitely his mama." She yawned to prove her point.

Regan cleared his throat. "I really like doing things with you and Tyler."

She felt the familiar flush but elected to overlook the familiarity of his words. "We enjoy having you along."

"Would. . ." He hesitated. "Would you consider doing something just with me?"

"Are you asking me for a date?"

"Uh, why yes, I am." At that moment, he reminded her of a shy schoolboy, stuttering through a rehearsed speech. "Is it a bad idea?" He shifted from one foot to the other.

"I don't know," she began. "I think I'd like to, but I feel like I'm betraying Vince."

He nodded and stared at the children in the petting arena. "I feel the same way about Carey and Brenna, and I've been praying about it."

"For how long?"

He sighed and offered a quick smile before casting his gaze back to the arena. "Since the day I saw you talking to Patrick at church."

He'd confused her. She couldn't remember anything out of the ordinary that Sunday. "Why then?"

"Not totally sure. Seemed like you suddenly looked different."

At the time I thought you looked odd. Could he have been. . . maybe jealous?

"Truthfully, I thought you two were, well, interested in each other."

"Oh, Regan." She laughed but quickly covered her mouth when she saw the seriousness etched on his face. "I'm sorry, but a relationship with anyone was the furthest thing from my mind. Besides, I hadn't made a rededication then."

Standing still, a bit of a chill wrapped around her, and she shivered.

"That's why I waited."

She nodded, not sure how to react. He's acting strange, or maybe it's me. "What did you have in mind—for a date I mean?"

"A movie or dinner or both."

Indecision swept over her. She hadn't thought of anyone but Vince for so long, but a part of her wanted to believe he'd approve. *Help me, Father. It's been so long since I walked with You that I must be sure.*

"Can I let you know on Tuesday night?" she finally asked. "I hope you see this is not an easy thing for me to consider."

"Oh, I understand. I haven't dated since Carey and Brenna died—never really wanted to until now."

Anita felt her insides tingle. "I'm flattered, another reason why I need to be sure the Lord wants me. . .more involved."

Regan waved at a shouting Tyler. "Makes me feel better you aren't taking this lightly, because I'm not."

❧

As tired as Anita felt, sleep escaped her. The weekend's activities had left her with a delicious delirium, a certain excitement laced with a twinge of fear. If she'd been looking for a handsome man, Regan fit the bill. His broad shoulders, sandy-colored hair, and steely blue eyes attracted many women, but she didn't care about those things. They faded with time. If she thought a man stood in her future, his heart would capture her above all things.

She simply couldn't jump into a possible relationship with Regan unless she knew for certain God intended it. And Tyler, how would he feel if she and Regan dated? He might not want to share his Big Brother with his mother. The turmoil in his little mind might undo all the work Regan had done to end the nightmares. Her son came first—his feelings and his welfare. She'd do anything for Tyler. Anything.

"Mom."

Anita started. He should have been asleep. "Yes, Honey."

He walked to her bed in the darkened room. "I don't feel so good."

Snapping on the light, she glanced into his pale face. "Did you have a bad dream?"

"No, my tummy hurts."

Too much fun today. "Do you want some of the pink medicine?" Tyler had a sensitive stomach and easily vomited.

"No, thanks. I hate that stuff." He nestled into her embrace, and she kissed his forehead.

"You must have eaten something your tummy didn't like."

"Probably." His words sounded like he knew exactly what had upset his stomach.

"Honey, what did you eat?" Her mind raced through lunch and dinner and a few snacks.

He snuggled closer. "Promise you won't get mad."

Oh, great. He must have gotten into Regan's candy stash. "I'll try not to. Right now, I need to know the truth in case we need to call the doctor."

"Well," Tyler began. "Remember the pellets we fed the animals?"

"Oh, no, you didn't. How much did you eat?" How would Regan react to this? Her thoughts were premature. He'd merely asked for a date, nothing else.

"Two pieces, but—

He broke away from her arms and raced to the bathroom. He'd once sampled dog food and nothing had come of it, but ingesting wildlife pellets could be a different story. She'd call the emergency room to be sure. Anita drew in a heavy breath and hurried after him.

She snapped on a light and snatched up a washcloth to dampen Tyler's head. Too late. The poor little guy hadn't made it to the bathroom in time. This would be a long night.

One more memorable account to put in his baby book.

❧

Regan read the newspaper article on the Harringer fire for the third time. Craig had initiated a personal interview to make sure he sounded like the victim. Anger surged through every inch of Regan as he read:

> *This community needs to know their homes and businesses are safe from arson. I pledge my time and efforts to the investigation until the offenders are brought to justice. I have a suspect, and the investigators are fully aware of this person's capabilities.*

Regan's stomach tightened. He flung the paper across his kitchen and watched it fall haphazardly on the floor. Did Craig think the citizens of Sweetwell were stupid enough to believe he'd now become a model citizen? That he had a suspect? At least he was smart enough not to mention Anita's name. Pastor Miller and the preschool board would be knocking on his door if he made that accusation. No doubt Craig had aimed his newspaper interview at his defense for the upcoming custody case and the charges from the preschool incident.

Won't work, Craig. The rest of us are smarter than you think. You've slipped somewhere along the line with the fire, and it's only a matter of time until we find the evidence needed to get you behind bars and away from the people you've harassed.

Leesa. The thought of Craig's daughter saddened Regan as it ushered in memories of Brenna. She'd been Leesa's age when she died—a beautiful, blond-haired little doll, always sweet, always the source of joy in her daddy's life. He'd walk through the fiery pits to see her wide-stretched arms seeking a hug, calling out for him to play. He remembered one Saturday morning in the park when she desperately wanted to venture down the "big kid's" slide, as she called it.

He remembered climbing the ladder with her and zooming down.

If Regan listened long enough, he could hear her squeals and the "Do it again, Daddy." When he least expected it, the baby-like scent of her wafted past him, plunging him into yesteryear. Oh, for the day when he crossed the portals of heaven and saw his tiny daughter. He knew for all eternity he'd see her and Carey in God's world of perfection. No fires. No death.

Yes, he understood completely how a father would attempt any feat to have contact with his child. But God didn't call parents to violence and degradation, and Craig must answer his accusers.

Regan's throat tightened, for now he'd called up another ghost of his past. Carey. The radiant bride, the loving wife, the devoted mother. Like ocean waves crashing against the shore, one memory after another assaulted him in snippets of days gone by but not forgotten.

Like Anita, he wondered if he'd betrayed Carey by seeking out a new relationship. Knowing his wife, she'd whisper no and with a sweet smile instruct him to go ahead with his life. From what Regan had heard about Vince Todd, he'd give the same advice to Anita.

God seemed to be leading him forward with Anita, but Regan felt like running in the opposite direction. Not that he doubted God's direction, he simply couldn't handle the cold chills and dry mouth syndrome when she looked his way. Her dark hair and olive-colored skin so characteristic of her Italian heritage, and the way she talked with her hands when excited drove him to distraction. Most everything about Anita drove him to distraction.

Wrapping his fingers around his mug of coffee, the third one that morning, Regan surmised Anita would decline his invitation. He nodded, assured of his conclusion. God must intend for them to establish a healthy brother-sister bond, without all the heart thumping stuff. The two of them could work together with genuine affection to help dissolve Tyler's nightmares.

The phone rang, and he slowly reached for it across the counter, not quite ready to relinquish his thoughts.

"Regan, this is Anita."

He hadn't expected her to call him, especially when she stood prominent in his mind. "Good morning."

"I thought you'd appreciate a bit of news about Tyler."

While he listened, she explained his nightlong illness and why Tyler believed it happened.

"What will he do next?" Regan chuckled. "I'm sorry. I know he's sick, and I feel sorry for him. Are you taking him to the doctor?"

"No, I think it's a bug, not the animal food. I'm going to have Mom watch him for me."

"Tell him I hope he feels better."

"Sure will. . . . Regan, I've been thinking about what you asked me yesterday."

He smiled. He'd calculated right, and soon his worries would be over.

"I've decided to accept your invitation."

sixteen

Anita heard a thud. "Did you drop the phone?" She heard another clatter and Regan mutter, "Great."

A moment later, he was back on the phone. "Uh, sorry, I dropped the phone the same time I took a drink of hot coffee, then I had to put it back together. You said okay to a date?"

"If you're still interested."

I can't believe she agreed.

"Sure. I'm surprised you gave me an answer so quickly."

She laughed. "Well, it came while taking Tyler to Mom's this morning."

"How's that?"

"He said if I ever wanted to have special time with you, it was okay with him. He thought I should have some fun too."

"Did you accuse him of conspiring with me?"

"Did you?"

"Nope. He's his own man. How about dinner and a movie or a movie and dinner, say Friday night?"

"Friday's fine, and in either order." She waved at a couple of teachers bustling through the front door of the school. A breeze whipped through the office with its reminder of fall's near arrival. "Sure glad Tyler is finished with soccer, the wind is vicious."

"I haven't been out yet, but I'm heading there soon. Gotta meet David at nine o'clock."

She sobered. "I'm praying the arsonist is found soon." A beep alerted her to an incoming call. "Oops, I've got to run."

"Thanks, and I want to talk to you about spending some time with Tyler on Tuesday evenings."

"We'll work out something. I'm praying his nightmares are finally over."

Anita replaced the phone just as Rhonda Harringer slouched through the door, gripping Leesa's hand. The woman's face was blotchy and swollen, her eyes bloodshot. Bad weekend.

"Good morning," Anita said. "Chilly morning."

Rhonda nodded. Her lips pressed together into a grim line. "I know I'm early, but I need to talk." She glanced about her. "Is someone available to watch Leesa?"

Anita inwardly cringed at the thought of asking one of the staff members to keep an eye on the little girl. These early morning minutes were precious to them all: planning, gathering supplies, paperwork. No, she didn't dare impose, and leaving a child alone in a room violated state laws.

"I'm a problem," Rhonda said, blinking back the tears.

Anita rose from her desk. She could only try. "Let's take a walk and see if any of the teachers are free." Not likely since it was Monday morning.

As suspected, every teacher and aide bustled about their rooms. Some were replacing learning centers for new hands-on projects, one teacher was spreading out butcher-block paper for a finger-paint project, and a kindergarten teacher was displaying different dried bugs in glass jars. The cook filled pitchers with water and concentrated juice for snack. She glanced up and offered Leesa a broad smile.

"Good morning, Leesa. You're early."

"I think Mommy wants to talk with Mrs. Todd," the precocious child said. She looked like Craig—aristocratic, graceful features, as though she'd stepped out of a seventeenth-century painting.

"You could pull up a chair to the kitchen door and talk to me."

Lord, bless my dear cook, Anita thought. "Thank you so much. Are you sure it's okay?"

"Mercy me. We'll keep each other company," the cook replied cheerfully.

Rhonda and Anita trailed back down the hall. The clock in her office registered thirty minutes before the children arrived. Anita led her to the break room where they'd have privacy. She pulled out a chair for the distraught woman.

"Sit down, Rhonda, and tell me what is going on in your life."

"I'm a wreck," she admitted. "Craig showed up yesterday afternoon while Leesa was playing outside. At least I was outside with her." She took a deep breath. "If I hadn't intervened, he'd have snatched her away."

Anita clenched her fists. The mere thought of anyone taking Tyler from her made her nauseous. "How did Leesa react?"

"Craig tried to coax her into coming with him. He promised candy and toys—the typical. I kept praying for strength and told her no. She cried, and when he saw the tears, he told her I was mean for not letting her leave with him." Rhonda took a deep breath, her thin shoulders sinking with despair.

"He started shouting and cursing at me, which scared Leesa into hysterics. My dear, sweet daughter promptly stood up for me, which infuriated him. One of the neighbors called the police, and they arrested Craig in front of Leesa." Rhonda's tears trickled down her cheeks. "He is her father, and I haven't ever discredited him in front of her."

"Sounds like he managed that on his own." Anita placed her arms around Rhonda's trembling shoulders.

"She'd never seen him in one of his tirades until yesterday. At one point, he stepped close and raised his hand to hit me, but her screams stopped him. Oh, Anita. He wouldn't let us by him to get to the house."

Anita wept with her. "Will he stay in jail until the trial next week?"

"I hope so. Patrick is doing all he can." She sniffed. "Can we pray together? You are the only friend I have. Any others I've had in the past, Craig ran off."

Uneasiness snaked up Anita's spine. She'd made her peace

with God, but praying aloud with Rhonda made her uneasy. "I. . .suppose we could. God will keep you and Leesa safe."

Rhonda closed her eyes and bowed her head, overwhelmed by a fresh surge of tears.

"Heavenly Father," Anita prayed, "we come to You frightened for Rhonda and Leesa. Keep them safe in the shelter of Your arms. The court hearing, Lord, is heavy on our minds. You know our hearts and what has happened in the past with Rhonda and Leesa's situation. Please touch Craig's heart and soften it for You. In Jesus' name, amen."

Anita held Rhonda until the sobs no longer shuddered through her body. Years had come and gone since Anita had comforted or prayed with anyone. The compassion and the realization that God had used her felt good—even if the circumstances were horrible. Shoving aside the doubts plaguing her, Anita vowed to begin memorizing Scripture again. She knew peace and strength rested in His Word.

Years ago, she'd developed the practice of writing Scripture on index cards, then attaching them on a ring and carrying them wherever she went. In spare moments, she read through them, cementing the Scripture in her heart. Determination spurred her to begin this practice again that evening.

The week flew by, hectic one minute and brimming with laughter the next. Children lived in a special world entwined with reality and fantasy. They utilized all their senses to explore everything from a singing red bird to a many-legged insect, from the silky feel of a dog's coat to the smells of baking pumpkin seeds. They eagerly crept into such a delightful place where she longed to slip and stay until the outside world promised only goodness. An impossibility, but the idea flowed inside her heart like honey trickling over a peanut butter sandwich.

Friday arrived before she had time to consider her date with Regan. Mid-afternoon, the thought hit her head on. She hadn't told a single soul but Mom. Come Monday morning,

Susan with her extra-sensory perception would know all about it.

Regan suggested going casual to an early movie and dinner afterward at a cozy restaurant known for its great barbecue. He certainly had acted strangely during the week. On Tuesday, she caught him staring at her as though she'd forgotten to comb her hair. On Thursday, he'd helped her put away dishes after she'd cooked dinner. He accidentally touched her hand and acted as if she'd burned him. She wondered if he regretted the invitation. Perhaps she should call him and get him off the hook. A nibble of irritation caused her to stiffen. *I'm not a charity case.*

Before losing her nerve, Anita punched in his cell number and listened to his voice mail. She hung up without leaving a message. *I think my nervousness has me overreacting. If tonight goes badly, I'll simply ask him to take me home.*

❧

At seven o'clock, Regan drove into the parking lot of Anita's apartment complex. His jitters had become an annoyance. *I can't believe I put myself through this during high school and college.* Any man who purposely planted himself into the trauma of dating deserved whatever happened to him.

Except he liked Anita—a lot. And if he took enough deep breaths, he'd relax and possibly enjoy himself. After parking his vehicle, he closed his eyes and leaned back against the seat. His stomach felt like Tyler's after he'd eaten animal food.

He forced one foot in front of the other and stepped out of his Jeep, his legs feeling like matchsticks.

I am a man. . . I have courage. . .

The moment she opened the apartment door, Regan knew he'd never be the same again. Dynamic best described her, or maybe perfection, or just downright gorgeous. He couldn't decide if what intrigued him centered around her thick hair bouncing off her shoulders, her pale blue eyes, or the black slacks hugging her trim figure—not too tight, not too oose—with a black-and-white striped sweater set. It must be he smile.

"You look great." He gulped. For a moment, he wanted to ear into his wallet and verify his age.

"Thanks. Come on in."

He glanced about. "Where's Tyler?"

"At Mom's. She had something special in mind for them."

He noticed she kept smiling. Ah, she had a case of the shakes too. "Are you as nervous as I am?"

Her shoulder bag slipped to her wrist. "Immensely. My mental capacity dropped to somewhere between high school and college."

They both laughed. "We are going to have fun," he said. "I promise."

The movie started out a bit dramatic, but it contained light-hearted moments where they could relax. Without thinking, Regan gathered up her hand. He appreciated the softness and the fact that she didn't yank it back. Still. . .

"Do you mind if I hold your hand?" he whispered.

"No," she replied. "You already are. Besides, Tyler said you might."

Startled, he raised a questioning brow. Anita covered her mouth; a giggle escaped her lips. "I figured you must have asked him."

He shook his head. "Tyler, the seven-year-old romantic."

❧

As soon as the waiter took their order, Anita realized she needed to conjure up some witty, date-like conversation. She'd be more than happy to do her share if she knew what to say. Country-western music thumped out a message about love, despair, and trucks. Laughter and voices ebbed around them in the dimly lit restaurant. These people had no problem opening their mouths and allowing words to fall out. But as she fidgeted in her chair and wished she'd turned down his invitation, stark reality marched across her mind. This was

Regan: her friend, the man who admittedly loved her son. Why in the world should she be anxious?

If she allowed herself to be totally honest, she liked Regan a lot, despite their rocky beginning and her misgivings about disappointing Vince. Regan's gaze met hers, and she felt drawn to the sincerity, the honesty, the integrity, and the gentleness emitting from his eyes.

"I'm glad we did this," he said, leaning an arm on the table.

"Me too." *At least I think so, if I could ever get over these jitters.*

"Why did we wait so long?" The sound of his voice reminded her of a country-western singer, half speaking, half talking his heartfelt message.

"I had issues."

He chuckled. "That's right."

Silence invaded them.

"Miss Todd! Miss Todd!"

Anita whipped her attention to a nearby table. A small boy waved wildly.

"Your fan club?" Regan asked in a whisper.

She nodded. "Hi, Jon. Are you having a good time?"

Jon pointed to his plate, his shoulders back and his chest puffed. "Dad says I'm eating like a horse."

"Wonderful," Anita replied with a laugh. "You have fun, and I'll see you on Monday." She glanced at Regan, who took a sip of water in an obvious attempt to keep from laughing.

"I see I must share you with all of Sweetwell."

She wiggled her shoulders. "Only the population under six." She searched for another topic—something intelligent and definitely adult. "How is work going, especially the arson investigation? Or would that be an inappropriate question?"

He shook his head and smiled. "Not at all. My job is always busy, and I really want to nail the firebug, excuse me. . . the pyromaniac."

"Your first analysis is more accurate. Do you honestly have a suspect?"

He reached across the table and gathered up her hand. His thumb gently massaged the top of her hand while he seemed completely absorbed in thought. "David and I believe we have a person who is highly capable of setting the fire. Trouble is we don't have enough evidence."

"Craig?" She purposefully kept her words soft. That man created such a terror in her that she often feared he might pounce on her from out of nowhere.

Regan shrugged. "I hate to spout how I feel. He's the type of guy who would use the information against me."

"I understand. Didn't mean to put you on the spot. For Rhonda and Leesa's sake, I'd like to see him out of town."

"You and a dozen others. When is her court case?"

"The first week of November." She reached for her water. Taking a sip, she continued, "Rhonda stopped into the office early two days this week. She needed to talk and wanted me to pray." Anita sighed. "Craig's harassing her again."

"Thought Patrick had taken care of his unpopular visits."

"He did, but his dad bailed him out of jail again."

Regan rubbed his chin. "I visited with Jacob on Wednesday. That man isn't about to leak out one bit of information. He advised me to seek out his attorney with my questions."

"Does Craig have an alibi?"

Regan frowned. "Says he was having dinner with his parents."

"And he's the only suspect?" Anita asked.

"The one and only."

The waiter set their salads before them. After offering freshly ground pepper and Parmesan cheese, he disappeared.

"Mind if I ask the blessing, Anita?" Since Regan already held her hand, his few words of prayer came easily. He released her hand and jabbed his fork into his salad. Suddenly she felt self-conscious of his scrutiny. Silently she questioned his stares.

"I want to talk about us," he said, moistening his lips. "Although the time's probably not right, I'm afraid if I don't say something soon, my courage will disappear."

Her heart plummeted. She preferred what she called "surface talking" to the serious stuff. Then they were merely friends; anything else made her seriously uncomfortable. Always in the back of her mind, she kept waiting for the doorbell to ring and Vince to be waiting on the other side. The past few years would dissolve into one bad dream. But lately she found Regan occupied more of her time and thoughts. Undoubtedly, Vince would have approved. He and Regan would probably have been buds.

"What's bothering you?" she finally managed. *I must dissuade him.* "Tyler being a pill, not minding?"

"Not at all." All manner of teasing had escaped his rugged features. "I like you, Anita, and I want to see more of you."

"But you do, with Tyler."

Lines creased his forehead. "You're not making this easy on me, are you?"

"I'm sorry." This type of coy behavior belonged to kids, not to a grown woman. "I need time, Regan; I'm a pretty cautious lady. Even you will have to admit my life has not been boring lately—some might even call it near catastrophic."

"We can take it slow." Every word echoed with tenderness.

"Snail's pace?" *Surely you understand how hard this is.*

"Whatever you say. Just keep me informed of the boundaries and chase me off when you're tired of me. If you'll agree to pray about it, that would make me extremely happy."

"I can, and I will. It's not you and me in the picture, but a little guy who already loves you."

Anita looked up at him shyly. Trust. She needed to trust God. Regan's suggestion felt so new, yet exciting. Almost forbidding. She never thought she'd love another man like Vince, and even if she learned to care for Regan, it wouldn't be the same. But it could be equally as rich a blessing.

"I do enjoy your company, very much." She picked through her baked potato as though her statement sounded like common knowledge.

"What more could I ask?" He grinned.

Anita noted his nervousness again but said nothing. *Poor man.*

"Of course I might ask for a good-night kiss."

She raised a brow.

"But I won't tonight, since it's our first date."

seventeen

Regan opened his office door, clearly surprised that Anita had stopped by for a visit. "You sure made my Monday," he said warmly.

Her pale face stopped him cold. Uneasiness snaked up his spine.

"Guess I've looked better," she managed. "Truthfully, I'm a notch higher than earlier in the day."

"Come on in, and let's talk."

She moistened her lips. "Are you sure you're not too busy?"

"Absolutely not."

She stepped in and slid into a chair across from his desk. *She's scared—and mad. What is going on?* Rather than sit at his desk, he pulled a chair beside her.

Anita offered a faint smile. "First of all, I want you to know I've already talked to Patrick about this. Since you are the fire marshal, I thought you should be the next to know."

"Know what?"

"I'm so angry I can barely think." She stiffened, and her lips quivered. "A subpoena was delivered to me this morning at the school. Looks like Craig's attorney convinced the police department that I had threatened him. I'm to be questioned about the warehouse fire."

Regan rose to his feet. "What?"

"Calm down, Regan." She glanced at her hand locked with his, then back to his face. "Craig has followed through with his accusation about me being responsible for the fire."

"That's nuts! Besides you have an alibi."

She shook her head. "The fire occurred around eleven o'clock, while Tyler and I slept. If I think about it, authorities

148

could claim I slipped out while Tyler slept."

Regan released her hand and paced the length of the room. "That is utterly ridiculous. Is he claiming you stole the key to the warehouse and knew his burglar alarm code?"

"Who knows? Looks like the incident at the preschool gave me a motive."

"That man has to be stopped." He pounded his fist on the desktop.

She nodded. "Hurry up. The idea of facing an arson charge makes me furious—and scared."

"I will get to the bottom of this, Anita, I promise."

❧

Anita held her breath as Rhonda emerged from her car. She had promised to stop by the preschool as soon as the judge ruled on her custody battle. Standing, Anita didn't know whether to run outside or attempt to convey some type of composure. She caught a glimpse of Rhonda's face. Smiling.

Unable to contain her joy any longer, Anita flung open the school's door and raced to her friend.

"We won!" Rhonda shouted, hugging Anita's shoulders. "Can you believe it? I have my baby, and Craig is not allowed near her." Her laughter turned to tears, and Anita shared in the same emotions.

"God is so good," Anita finally said, swiping a tear. "Come inside and have a cup of coffee."

Rhonda hurried in with her. A nasty chill whipped around and caught them unaware. "I can't stay very long, and I can't even tell Leesa the good news, but I am blessed, sincerely blessed."

"Now you can go back to living a normal life."

Rhonda opened the office door for them. "Not really, Anita. I will have to leave town and move somewhere where Craig can't find us. I'm afraid, despite the court order, he will always seek Leesa. His parents don't want me to go, but they said they understand."

"Must it be that way?" But Anita knew the answer to her question the moment she uttered the words. "I guess it's the price you have to pay."

"I have an idea where we can go. All I need to do is make sure work is available for me."

Anita smiled. "Wonderful. Let's brew a fresh pot of coffee and relax for a few minutes."

Thank You, Lord, for giving Rhonda and Leesa another chance of happiness. May You always shelter them in Your unfailing love.

❧

The air suddenly changed from crisp to cold, and Anita wished she'd worn her coat instead of a jacket to work. At least it was Saturday, and she could wear her jeans. Two weeks until Thanksgiving, and she needed to make sure holiday plans and crafts were on target for the rest of the year.

Regan had offered to help, but she preferred to spend quality time with him later. How pleasantly odd. The more she saw of him, the more her emotions heightened. This week, she'd done a lot of thinking and praying about Regan, and she found herself getting very comfortable with the idea of him in her and Tyler's life. Her feelings might not be love just yet, but they were a very strong like. Very strong. Maybe love after all.

Pulling her car up in front of the preschool's door, she quickly ushered Tyler outside. She had the foresight to insist he wear a jacket; too bad she didn't have enough sense to heed her own advice.

"I'm going to put my roller blades on inside, okay Mom?" Tyler slung his skates over his shoulder by the laces.

"Sure. Don't you think it's too cold?"

"Nope. I have to be in shape for when Mr. Regan comes over this afternoon and we all go skating."

Anita grinned and tousled his hair. "Okay, Sweetie. You skate while I finish my paperwork. I won't be long, and if you do some great stunt on your roller blades, I'll see you from the window."

Tyler gave her a serious thumbs-up.

Moments later, she was humming a tune along with the radio on her desk. Every now and then, she took a look at Tyler whizzing back and forth on the parking lot much faster than she preferred. His thick dark hair blew straight back as if he dared defy the wind. His resemblance to Vince snatched her breath, but not in a melancholy way as it once did. She'd always have a piece of Vince in her heart and in his son.

Back at work, she processed a new child's application, entering the data into her computer. She had an opening in the three-day-a-week preschool class, which suited the parents perfectly. The sound of a vehicle seized her attention. She glanced up to see a small green sedan pull up alongside Tyler.

Apprehension jolted her to her feet. A familiar figure emerged from the car. Her heart raced. The chair toppled to the floor. Out the door. She had to get to Tyler. She tripped on the pavement. Scrambling to her feet, she raced toward her son.

Anita knew the man for certain. Craig Harringer.

He sneered at her, then waved. In the next instant, he grabbed Tyler and threw him into the back seat. The car squealed as Craig slammed it into reverse. He gunned the engine and tore out of the parking lot, taking Tyler with him.

"No." Her screams echoed around her.

❧

Regan barely heard his cell ring. As much as he detested cleaning, Anita and Tyler were headed his way this afternoon for a roller-blading session. All morning he'd vacuumed, cleaned bathrooms, wiped down the kitchen, and even dusted.

"Hello, Regan here." He couldn't make out the caller for the muffled sobs. A shiver raced up his spine. "Anita."

"He's gone," she cried. "Tyler's gone."

Fear pounded against his brain. "What do you mean? Slow down, what's happened?"

He heard her gasp. "He was. . .skating in front of the school. I–I heard a car." Her sobs increased. "Craig Harringer. He snatched Tyler and drove away."

Regan frantically searched for his keys. "The police."

"They're here. I got the license number. It all happened too fast. Please come, Regan. Please."

"I'm on my way. And pray, keep praying. I'm not hanging up; keep talking to me." Craig must be drowning in desperation. He'd lost his daughter, and Tyler could be his last hope to get Leesa—leverage. *Dear Lord, not Tyler. Keep him safe until we can find him.*

When a few minutes later he whipped into the school's parking lot, Regan's attention flew to Anita. She leaned against a police car beside his friend Jordan, her arms wrapped around her chest, one hand holding her cell phone, her head drooped to her chest. She'd hung up to call her mother and hadn't called him back. If anything could squash her rededication to the Lord, this would. Faith. Trust. Regan couldn't exist another day without it, but could Anita?

As he hurried to her, Theresa spun into the parking lot. Praise God. This lady knew how to handle emergencies. Anita remained in her beaten stance. *Come on, Sweetheart. Pray, don't withdraw.*

"Anita," he whispered. She lifted her head, and he took her into his arms. Uncontrollable weeping burst from her trembling body. "My baby," she sobbed. "Why did God do this? Hasn't He hurt me enough?"

Regan held her close, stroking her back as though she were a child. "God didn't do this," he said. "What happened today is wrong, evil. He's not to blame for this."

"He could have stopped it. Instead He did nothing while that animal kidnaped my son." Her words echoed the same sentiments he'd once felt about his family. A few years ago he'd come to a realization that while God is in control of everything in this world, evil still abounds—whether the wrongdoings are acts of wicked men or unexplainable tragedies. But now was not the right time to explain his findings to Anita. Right now she needed to grieve.

"I know. I understand." He pulled her from his chest and peered into her face, tear stained and swollen. "Let me pray with you, Honey. We have to trust God to keep Tyler safe."

"Look what happened when I trusted God!" Anger seethed from every pore of her skin; sheer panic echoed from her eyes. "I've been betrayed for the last time." She lowered her face. "I don't want to live without Tyler."

Regan shook her slightly, and when her reddened eyes met his in retribution, he said. "Don't talk this way. We have to believe the police will find Tyler, and I'm praying for that very thing."

Theresa stood a few feet away, watching, her normally calm composure shaken, her face as pale as Anita's. Regan met her gaze with a degree of helplessness. She lifted her chin with an air of determination.

"Anita," she whispered, stepping closer. Regan released his hold and allowed Theresa to gather her daughter into her arms.

Regan turned to Jordan, who had his attention focused on an incoming call. Regan heard enough to know Craig's car had been found.

"What do you know?" He hoped and prayed the found vehicle also contained Tyler.

Jordan frowned and curled his upper lip, his dark features indicating his disgust. "Harringer wasted no time in abandoning his car. At this point, we're trying to figure out what he's driving, where he's headed. Mrs. Todd gave us a description of what her son was wearing and a picture."

Craig's daddy can't bail him out of this one. "Anyone contacted Jacob?"

The policeman nodded. "We've got a man on it."

Regan searched his friend's face, looking for something—a clue, good news, or possibly the worst. "So what's next?"

"We look until we find something. In the meantime, Mrs. Todd will most likely get a phone call from Harringer. I imagine he has a list of demands."

Regan cast his attention on Anita to see if she'd heard Jordan's remark. She broke away from Theresa's embrace; the ashen look on her face spoke fathoms.

"Mrs. Todd, why don't you go on home and stay near a phone? We'll be in contact."

"But I have to do something," she protested.

"I'll take her," Theresa said, wrapping her arm around her daughter's waist.

"I'll wrap up things here and be there shortly." Regan gave Theresa a supportive nod, then watched the two women get into Theresa's car. *Oh, Lord, please keep Tyler safe.*

&

At her apartment, Anita refused to rest or take a sedative. Her muddled thoughts jumped from her last conversation with Tyler to the many atrocities of Craig Harringer and on to the day when Vince had had his accident. She willed the phone to ring, believing the police would locate her son at anytime. Her mind spun so fast she refused to talk, or rather she couldn't. She paced in front of the huge bay window facing the street.

No one had seen or heard from Craig, not even his father, or so he claimed. The police department said they'd keep her informed. She'd been given specific instructions if Craig should call demanding ransom. Cooperate. Keep in control. Learn all she could about their whereabouts. The police had tapped her phone line, but she'd have to keep Craig on the phone for a few minutes in order to trace the call.

How could God have done this to her again?

The hours trickled by. Regan stayed with her, although she didn't know why. Her anger was aimed at him too. After all, his God had done nothing to prevent this.

"I shouldn't have left him outside alone," she finally said, her words choked with emotion.

"Weren't you watching him through the office window?" her mother asked, first sitting, then standing, and always wringing her hands as though squeezing out her own emotions.

"Yes, but it didn't stop Craig from snatching him." Anita's words sounded distant to her, as if someone else spoke them. Her ears rang. Had she truly gone insane?

"Pray," her mother said. "That's all we can do."

Anita wanted to scream, to tell her mother that God didn't care. Look at what He'd done. His idea of love slammed her heart into a standstill. Enough. All she could do was count on the police to find Craig before he hurt Tyler.

"Why don't I ask Pastor Miller to come by? He's called a few times," Mom suggested.

"No!" Anita shouted. "I don't want or need anyone shoving religion down my throat." With those words, she fled to her room and slammed the door. Now she was truly alone. She had no one, not her mother or Regan. The two people she knew cared for her. She dissolved into a pool of tears on her bed, sobbing, pleading to whoever was in control to bring back her son safe.

A hand caressed her back. She stiffened, recognizing the scent of the one who invaded her privacy.

"Don't ask me to leave," Regan whispered. "Because I don't intend to step one foot outside of this apartment until Tyler is found. I am here for you."

Unable to look at him, she stared at the picture of Vince and Tyler together. Helpless and frightened, the tears continued to flow. "I know you love Tyler too."

"I love both of you." Those words, if she'd heard them earlier, would have enveloped her in happiness. Now they fell empty. Nothing else mattered. He massaged her shoulders. While his touch offered a sense of comfort, she felt empty, lifeless.

"Don't cast God aside. I believe He is wanting us to trust Him."

"I can't," she said. "Why does He do this to me?"

"He doesn't, Sweetheart. Can I read something to you?"

She didn't respond. It seemed as though her anger and fight had suddenly melted in the same pool as her sorrow. "I understand you mean well and you believe—"

"And so do you, Anita. You feel as though your heart has been yanked from your body. I know that feeling, but I know God listens and cares. Let Him comfort you with His Word and His peace."

Deep inside she realized the truth of Regan's words. "I want to put the blame somewhere. Someone has to be accountable for this."

"It's the depravity of a man's mind," he said. "Not God. Craig chose his behavior. The law and God will deal with him."

She said nothing, the well inside of her soul became deeper and deeper. Swallowing her tears, she turned to him. "Help me, Regan. I'm so scared."

He held her close as before, except this time she heard his sobs. His sorrow in some strange way gave her strength to hold onto him tighter. Regan loved her; he loved Tyler. Yes, she'd listen to him. If God had strengthened Regan, surely something could be done for her. She wanted to be wrong and for the heartache in her life not to be God's fault. As they clung to each other, she remembered her joy in following the Lord and the emptiness in deserting Him. She didn't really want to abandon Him now. She simply wanted Tyler back and justice done to Craig.

"Go ahead and read to me," she whispered. "My Bible is on the nightstand." She took a deep breath. "Regan, I feel like the man in the Bible who wanted Jesus to cure his child, the one who said, 'Help my unbelief.'"

He kissed her forehead, a kiss of comfort, and again her eyes brimmed. She felt his gaze sweep over her face. *If I could only feel God's love the way I feel Regan's now. If I could only be assured God has sent His angels to protect my son.*

Regan opened Anita's Bible, the one that had once belonged to her and Vince. "When my life was shattered, and my parents and those around me tried to comfort me, I realized those few peaceful moments disappeared the moment I was alone again. In desperation, I searched the Scriptures and prayed for a passage to call mine—a Word from God describing His love for me and assuring me I would make it through the pain." He offered her a smile. "It's from Isaiah, chapter 61."

A fresh onslaught of tears poured over her cheeks. "That was Vince's chapter. He'd been abused as a child, and those verses spoke to him, convinced him of God's love and mercy. When I decided to stop my bitterness and return to the Lord, those verses gave me hope."

"Strange with all the verses in the Bible that we are drawn to the same ones, but I don't believe in coincidences, just divine appointments from God." He clasped her hand as he leafed through the pages. "Verses 1 and 2 say: 'He has sent me to bind up the brokenhearted, to proclaim freedom for the captives and release from darkness for the prisoners, to proclaim the year of the Lord's favor and the day of vengeance of our God, to comfort all who mourn, and provide for those who grieve in Zion—to bestow on them a crown of beauty instead of ashes, the oil of gladness instead of mourning, and a garment of praise instead of a spirit of despair.' "

How different the verses sounded coming from Regan. He'd been in a similar abyss and risen above the despair. Prayer. Communion with God. These were her answers.

"Tyler hasn't had a nightmare since you two prayed about it together two months ago. I wonder if the difference is the fact that he believed God would take them away." She blinked away the wetness lingering on her lashes. "I have to grab hold of the same faith and not let go."

"You can do it," Regan whispered. "All of us want to

help—all of us who love you." He hesitated. "Surely you must know by now how much I love you and Tyler."

He'd said the love word again. Such an odd time for affairs of the heart to plant themselves in the middle of chaos.

"Right now I can only think about my son. Anything else will have to wait."

"I understand." He released a heavy sigh. "I didn't mean to put you into an awkward position, only let you know my feelings."

She nodded and stood from the bed. "Right now I need to be strong and believe in God and the people around me." Placing her hand on his cheek, she prayed to be the woman God intended. "I have to talk to Mom. I know she's miserable." She stepped to the door, feeling strangely stronger, and opened it. "Mom, do you suppose Pastor Miller would come over and stay with us for awhile? I believe we all could use the prayers."

Her mother looked years older, nearly haggard, but Anita's words brought a fresh smile to her face. "I'm sure he'd be delighted. I already know he's called for a community prayer meeting this evening for Tyler."

Anita moved to her mother and kneeled at her side. "I'm sorry for the things I said."

Her mother kissed her forehead. "I know, Honey. We all are hurting, but we can't give up."

"It's so hard not to be bitter," Anita admitted. "I want Craig found and punished."

"I feel the same way, but we need to leave the punishing to God and the judicial system."

Anita closed her eyes and willed away the tears. "I simply want Tyler found—unharmed."

eighteen

An hour later, while Pastor Miller sat with Anita, her mother, and Regan, the six o'clock TV news from Tulsa announced the kidnaping. They described Tyler and Craig and aired pictures of them both. Anita's mother changed to an Oklahoma City broadcast and found the same report. She made a few phone calls and learned Dallas and local TV programs were doing the same.

"This is more than a few simple policemen looking for a small boy," Pastor Miller stated. "My guess is that the whole state and surrounding area are involved, possibly the FBI too."

Pastor Miller stayed through the night, shifting his responsibilities to another pastor to lead the community prayer vigil. Never had Anita felt so loved. The peace she craved showered on her in an incredible, supernatural way. The hysteria vanished. The need to comfort others and assure them of their faith sprung from her like an overflowing fountain. Tyler would be found safe and unharmed. She must believe it.

After midnight, the phone stopped ringing. Mom, Pastor Miller, and Regan snoozed off and on, but she couldn't. Instead she stared at the phone and waited.

"Anita, why don't you try to get a little rest?" Regan said quietly. Her mother had stretched out on her bed, and the pastor slept in a stuffed chair. "You know we'd wake you with any information."

She picked up her coffee. Its bitter taste kept her awake. "I can't. When I have my arms around Tyler, I can relax, but until then I must be alert." He scooted to the end of the sofa where she sat and wrapped his arm around her shoulders.

Her head leaned against his chest. "You haven't slept much at all either."

"We're in this together, remember?"

She snuggled close to him. Why had it taken this tragedy for her to realize how much she loved Regan? Later she'd tell him, when Tyler was found. *Oh, Lord, remember my baby. Keep him safe and bring him back to us.* A tear trickled down her cheek, and Regan wiped it off. She peered up into his face and saw his eyes moisten too. *Lord, I have failed to see this is reminding him of his loss. How selfish of me.*

The hours passed slowly until dawn. At five o'clock, Pastor Miller stirred. "I need to head home and get cleaned up. I have a sermon to deliver this morning."

Regan moaned. "I hadn't even considered today being Sunday. You must be exhausted."

"Oh, I'll be fine. I've slept a lot. Just need to shower and look respectable."

The poor man, Anita thought. "I'll make some fresh coffee and put together some breakfast for you," she said through sleep-laden eyes.

"That's out of the question." Pastor Miller stood and massaged his back. "I'll be back after the service, probably around noon. In the meantime, if you hear anything, call me on my cell." When she started to protest, he shook his head. "I know I tell everyone on Sunday mornings to turn those things off, but today is an exception."

"Thank you, Pastor." Anita stood to walk him to the door.

"Please, I can find my way out." He grasped her hand. "We'll all continue praying."

She nodded and blinked back the tears. Why hadn't the authorities called or found some sort of clue? They didn't even know what kind of car Craig was driving.

After the pastor left, Anita walked into Tyler's room. She hadn't been able to bring herself to enter any earlier. Maybe she wanted to believe he was in bed sleeping.

"Are you sure you want to be in here?" Regan leaned against the door.

"I think so. I need to touch his things, feed his hamster." She shrugged. "Lay out his clothes for Sunday school and church."

"Anita, don't torture yourself."

She turned to peer into his face. "And what would you do?"

His shoulders slumped. "The same thing."

She opened the blinds so when the sun rose, its light would brighten his room. Tyler's little Bible lay on his dresser with a bookmark. She turned to the marked page. Daniel and the lion's den. Swiping a tear, she handed the open book to Regan.

"Have I ever shown you his baby pictures?" Her lips quivered. *How much longer, Lord?*

"No, but I'd like to see them." He set the Bible back in its place and took her hand. "If you'll get the pictures, I'll make fresh coffee."

The morning dragged on. Mom offered to make breakfast, but no one had an appetite. After she insisted they eat something, Anita and Regan conceded to toast. Their last meal had been breakfast the day before.

Late that morning, Pastor Miller returned. Dark shadows ribbed beneath his eyes, and the lines in his face looked deeper. "Everyone is praying," he said. "Some are bringing food here after church."

"We do have wonderful people at Good Hope." Mom attempted to smooth her ruffled blouse. "I'm really thankful."

"I am too," Anita agreed, adding, "We've heard nothing except that the FBI is assisting in the search." She ached all over, but mostly in her heart.

The pastor pulled an envelope from his pocket. "Don't know quite how to present this. Jacob Harringer gave it to me after church."

She took the envelope, not convinced she wanted to view its contents. Slowly, her fingernail loosened the flap. A single piece of paper with a hand-written note fell to the floor.

Regan picked it up, and when she took the paper she wondered why Craig's father would write her. Moistening her lips, she elected to read it aloud:

> *Mrs. Todd—*
>   *Words cannot express the sorrow I feel today in light of your missing son. I am to blame. I know that. All of Craig's life I've spoiled him, thinking this was the way for him to see God. How wrong I've been. Even when I shut off his funds after he hurt Rhonda, I gave in to bail him out of jail. I'm a miserable failure as a father, and I pray God forgives me.*
>   *I want to do whatever I can to help you. Money is no object. If he demands money, I'll pay every cent. If he contacts me, I'll alert the police.*
>   *Something else too. I want you to be the first one to know that Craig was not with me and his mother the night of the warehouse fire. My guess is he's bullied his secretary into keeping her mouth shut. I need to face the possibility he's most likely guilty of arson too. Again, my sincere apologies for my son's behavior.*
>   *Jacob Harringer*

Anita slipped the note into the envelope and laid it on the coffee table. "He's riddled with guilt."

Mom pursed her lips. "Jacob just didn't know how to properly love that boy. He thought care and nurturing meant shielding Craig from all the consequences of his bad choices. His mother is the same way. I'd gladly stand in the way of a truck heading toward Anita, but I'm the first in her face when she's wrong."

"Rightfully so." Anita offered a weak smile. "You must love me a lot. Thanks, and I love you." She hugged her mom, fighting the tears and clinging to her for strength.

Oh, Lord, I simply want a chance to let Tyler know how

much I love him—ground him when he makes a mistake, hold him next to me, be a den mother, cheer at his soccer games. Please, Lord, bring him back to me.

Anita pulled away from her mom and glanced at Regan, realizing his thoughts were not on the arson case but on Tyler. "Now you have your suspect. When we find Tyler, Craig will be behind bars for a long time."

He slowly nodded. "I don't want a single person hurt again by Craig's self indulgence, and now I believe Jacob feels the same."

Shortly after noon, several families stopped by with food and words of encouragement. They declined invitations to enter the apartment, as though they knew the occupants would have a difficult time being hospitable.

As the afternoon wore on, Anita and Regan slept fitfully on the sofa. At least she didn't have to concern herself with school; the pastor had made arrangements to have the front office covered. Just before six, she made a decision. "Mom, I'm going to shower and change clothes. If anything happens, please let me know."

The hot water against her back sent tiny needles into her flesh. Any other time, she'd relished the warmth of a long shower. Not today. Every moment ticking by increased her anxiety. She didn't dare think about Craig hurting Tyler. He couldn't be that deranged, could he?

The evening shadows escorted the darkness, and with it the apprehension of another long night. While most of the city and state slept, the search for Tyler Todd continued. The news stations repeated the broadcasts. At one point, the police investigators paved the way for Anita to appear on various networks to plead for her son. The interview would be early in the morning. Anita realized the longer the span of time, the more the likelihood of Craig doing harm to Tyler. She didn't dare dwell on the horrible possibilities.

She couldn't eat, she couldn't sleep, only pray.

Shortly after seven the following morning, the TV cameras arrived. Exhaustion pulled on Anita, yet she believed in what she was doing. The reporter chose the parking lot of the apartment building for the taping.

"Tyler, wherever you are, this is Mommy, and I want you to know how much I love and miss you." Tears washed over her cheeks. "Craig, please, I beg you, release my son. Whatever you want, I'll get for you, just let me have my son safe."

The reporter interjected. "Mrs. Todd, what are you doing to strengthen your hope in this tragedy?"

She swallowed and nearly choked. "Only my faith in God, His peace, keeps me going. I trust He will not allow anything to happen to my son."

The reporter went on to speak about the community of Sweetwell holding prayer vigils and offering their support. Anita tuned out the rest of the report; her mind had grown numb. She allowed Regan to guide her back into the apartment building.

Late that morning, she resumed her position on the sofa—her ears listening for the phone and her gaze fixed to the TV. The phone rang. Anita snatched it up, her heart beating relentlessly against her chest. It was Pastor Miller's wife wanting to know if she could do anything.

"No, thank you," Anita repeated, feeling like a wind-up doll conditioned to be polite no matter what raged around her.

Monday afternoon crawled into evening. No word. Nothing but the emptiness of her heart.

๑

Regan watched the streetlights outside of Anita's apartment stand as sentries for the few people who passed by. Somewhere out there a child needed a light to find his way home. This, the third evening of Tyler's disappearance, Regan waited and prayed for God to spare the boy.

Anita appeared to sleep on the sofa, the phone at her fingertips. Exhausted, she refused to lie down in bed. She would only lean against a pillow anchored against the sofa rest. Regan no longer knew what to say to comfort her, especially when he felt hope slipping through his fingers.

"Can we step outside?" Pastor Miller whispered from the lounge chair.

Regan nodded, and the two eased toward the door into the cooler temperatures of the night. Once the door closed, Pastor Miller leaned against the metal railing.

"We can't give up," he said softly.

Regan wet his lips. "It's easier said than actually holding onto faith." He joined the pastor at the railing.

"We also need to think about the possibilities of Tyler not surviving."

"I've been trying not to think about that aspect, but I guess we need to discuss it." Regan closed his eyes. How could so little time mean so much?

Pastor Miller rubbed his face and chin. "I'm not suggesting we give up, only that we need to face the fact God may have other plans. Anita will need all of us if that is the case."

"I understand." *Oh, Father, this would crush her.*

વે

Anita had heard the outside door of the apartment open and sensed Regan and Pastor Miller stood outside talking. She didn't want to know their conversation. She feared it. For by hearing their muffled words, she might be forced to face something more evil than she could fathom. A sinister whisper spoke to her: Tyler might have joined Vince.

વે

A tomb. Anita felt her apartment had become a chamber of choked emotions and numbness. Glancing at her mother, then to Regan and Pastor Miller, she wondered how much longer they could go on. She'd prayed for so long; it seemed there was nothing left inside her but emptiness. Tuesday morning still had brought no answers.

She couldn't eat. She couldn't sleep, and her body weakened

as the clock ticked by the long moments. She refused to discuss the fears haunting her, and likewise, she'd refused to allow any type of conversation about various outcomes of the situation.

The phone rang, and each time her heart threatened to burst through her chest. But now, she wondered if she really wanted to hear the news.

Tuesday evening, she tried a few crackers and applesauce. Wednesday, the press asked for another interview, and she gave it. She sent Pastor Miller home. Regan stayed along with her mother. Silence held its mixture of blessings and sorrow.

Thursday morning, she wept while she showered, always listening for the phone. Late that morning, while the pastor visited, it rang.

"Mrs. Todd. This is the Tulsa police. We have your son."

Tears stung her eyes, and she tried desperately to swallow them, stop them, so she could speak.

"Mrs. Todd?"

"Yes. Yes, I'm here. Is he okay?"

Immediately Regan, her mother, and the pastor crowded around her.

"He's fine. In fact he's right here beside me."

"Can I talk to him, please?"

She heard the phone shuffle. *Thank You, Jesus. Thank You.*

"Mom. It's me. I'm okay and ready to come home."

She couldn't speak for the lump in her throat. "I'm. . .I'm so glad. Are you sure you're not hurt?"

"Yes. Mr. Craig didn't hurt me. He said he didn't have a little girl anymore and wanted me to be his little boy."

Her tears continued, but as quickly as they fell, she whisked them away. "Thank You, Jesus," slipped from her lips.

"I prayed for you, Mom. I knew you'd be scared. When can I come home?"

"Let me talk to the policeman." She could hear Tyler give the phone to the officer.

"I can leave here in a few minutes for Tulsa," she said

through a ragged breath. "He has no marks? Has he eaten?"

"We'll take good care of him until you arrive, and we'll also have a doctor take a look at your son, but he's okay."

"And Harringer?"

"We have him in custody. Seems like a woman recognized him and your son at a convenience store early this morning."

"Let me give you my cell phone number, and I want yours. I want to leave right away." Anita scribbled down the police station's phone number and replaced the phone. "He's safe and unharmed. Thank You, Lord, thank You. He's at a police station in Tulsa." She stepped into Regan's arms, her joyful tears soaking his shirt.

The phone rang again, and Mom answered. "Thank you," she said through her tears. "God bless you." She turned to Anita, choking back the sobs. "That was Jacob Harringer. Somehow he heard about finding Tyler. He's offered his helicopter and pilot for you to pick up Tyler."

nineteen

Anita waited for the helicopter to fuel up. The task seemed to take an eternity. Twice she'd talked to Tyler on the phone, and he sounded tired. Once they were home, the two of them could sleep peacefully. He'd probably need some Christian counseling after this ordeal, but she knew God was in control. Her eyes pooled, this time out of gratitude. *Thank You. Thank You for listening to a mother's cry.* Anita turned to Regan; the time had come.

"I love you," she managed through a ragged breath. She stole a glimpse into his endearing eyes. "You've tried to mirror Jesus to me, even when I didn't deserve it. I can't deny what your presence has done for me and my son. When this is over, could we. . ."

"Talk about something more permanent?" Regan's gentleness brought a fresh sprinkling of tears.

She nodded. "Next to God, you're my best friend."

☙

From the helicopter window, Anita stared down at the vehicles below: three police cars, a van from the *Tulsa World*, vans and cars bearing the logos of TV and radio stations, and a host of other cars, but her gaze stayed fixed on one little boy standing between two policemen. Tyler.

"It will only be a few minutes," Regan said.

"It can't be fast enough."

He squeezed her hand gently, and she tore her gaze to offer a tear glazed smile. "I don't want to cry when I see him, but I can't stop."

"Honey, you laugh, cry, shout, do whatever you feel because I'll be right there doing the same thing."

The helicopter descended and within moments had stopped; the deafening, whirling noise finally ceased. Throwing off the seat belt, she waited impatiently for the pilot to exit and open the door.

No sooner had Anita's feet touched the pavement than the policemen began escorting Tyler toward her. One held her son's hand, as though ensuring her of their utmost protection until she could hold him.

"Mom!" Tyler shouted, and the policeman released him. His short legs raced to meet her.

She ran toward Tyler, his arms flung wide and a tousle of dark curls picking up the afternoon sun.

"Mom!" he cried again as she lifted him into her embrace. The touch and smell of him, the taste of his cheek against her lips, brought on blinding tears.

"I missed you so much," he said amidst his own tears.

Ignoring the reporters and their incessant questions, she could only cling to the little body wrapped around hers. She knew Regan needed to hold him too, but for now she couldn't let go. "Let's go home," she whispered. Trembling, she peered into the chocolate brown eyes and pulled him close again. "Thank You, Lord. Thank You."

❧

"Have you two been eating licorice again?" Anita pretended annoyance. Regan and Tyler had black lips, and she felt certain their tongues were the same nasty shade.

"What makes you think that?" Regan grinned, displaying stained teeth.

"Yeah, Mom. We chewed it up and swallowed it all before we got here."

She brimmed with love for the two men in her life and found herself laughing at their antics.

"We were celebrating," Regan went on to say. He closed the apartment door behind him, a broad smile and twinkling eyes captured her curiosity.

"And what were you celebrating?" she asked.

Tyler wrapped his arms around her waist. "You tell her, Mr. Regan. It's your job. Today you're the man."

She raised a questioning brow. "I'm ready. What's going on?"

"Do you remember the mark of the black lips?" Regan jammed his hands into his jeans pocket.

And do I? "I have a faint recollection of the saying."

He reached over and gave her a light kiss on the lips.

Tyler groaned. "Mr. Regan, I'd have done it on her cheek. Gross." He glanced up at his mom. "Yep, it's black all right. Good sign."

"Hmm. Must mean I love your mom."

Anita giggled. "You two are a case. All right, I give. I love you both. So what is this all about?"

Regan pulled a tiny box from his pocket. A black velvet box. Her eyes widened, and she covered her mouth to stifle the growing anticipation.

"Tyler gave me the okay for what I'm about to ask." Regan opened the box and rested it in the palm of his hand. "Since he approves, I need to ask you something very important."

Tyler giggled. "A proposal. See, I remembered what it was called."

Anita sank her gaze into those steely blue eyes. She saw the familiar warmth and tenderness, his compassion for life, and his love for God.

Regan dropped to one knee and took her hand into his. His hand felt cold, clammy. Tyler giggled, but she didn't look his way. Her legs felt like jelly, and her heart pounded overtime.

"Anita, would you? I mean I'm asking you to marry me and spend the rest of your life with me."

She blushed for she also saw a fire blazing in his eyes, one she never intended to put out.

A Letter To Our Readers

Dear Reader:

In order that we might better contribute to your reading enjoyment, we would appreciate your taking a few minutes to respond to the following questions. We welcome your comments and read each form and letter we receive. When completed, please return to the following:

Rebecca Germany, Fiction Editor
Heartsong Presents
PO Box 719
Uhrichsville, Ohio 44683

1. Did you enjoy reading *Licorice Kisses* by DiAnn Mills?
   ❑ Very much! I would like to see more books by this author!
   ❑ Moderately. I would have enjoyed it more if

   _____

   _____

   _____

2. Are you a member of **Heartsong Presents**? ❑ Yes ❑ No
   If no, where did you purchase this book? _____

   _____

3. How would you rate, on a scale from 1 (poor) to 5 (superior), the cover design? _____

4. On a scale from 1 (poor) to 10 (superior), please rate the following elements.

   _____ Heroine   _____ Plot
   _____ Hero   _____ Inspirational theme
   _____ Setting   _____ Secondary characters

6. How has this book inspired your life?_____

_____

_____

7. What settings would you like to see covered in future
   Heartsong Presents books? _____

_____

_____

8. What are some inspirational themes you would like to see
   treated in future books? _____

_____

_____

9. Would you be interested in reading other **Heartsong
   Presents** titles? ❏ Yes ❏ No

10. Please check your age range:
    ❏ Under 18   ❏ 18-24
    ❏ 25-34   ❏ 35-45
    ❏ 46-55   ❏ Over 55

Name_____

Occupation _____

Address _____

City_____ State_____ Zip_____

E-mail_____

SEATTLE

Shepherd of Love Hospital stands as a beacon of hope in Seattle, Washington. Its Christian staff members work with each other—and with God—to care for the sick and injured. But sometimes they find their own lives in need of a healing touch.

Can those who heal find healing for their own souls? How will the Shepherd for whom their hospital is named reveal the love each one longs for?

Contemporary, paperback, 480 pages, 5 ³⁄₁₆" x 8"

❤ ❤ ❤ ❤ ❤ ❤ ❤ ❤ ❤ ❤ ❤ ❤ ❤

❤ ❤ ❤ ❤ ❤ ❤ ❤ ❤ ❤ ❤ ❤ ❤ ❤

Heartsong

CONTEMPORARY ROMANCE IS CHEAPER BY THE DOZEN!

Buy any assortment of twelve *Heartsong Presents* titles and save 25% off of the already discounted price of $3.25 each!

*plus $2.00 shipping and handling per order and sales tax where applicable.

Any 12 Heartsong Presents titles for only $30.00*

HEARTSONG PRESENTS TITLES AVAILABLE NOW:

Presents

Great Inspirational Romance at a Great Price!

Heartsong Presents books are inspirational romances in contemporary and historical settings, designed to give you an enjoyable, spirit-lifting reading experience. You can choose wonderfully written titles from some of today's best authors like Hannah Alexander, Andrea Boeshaar, Yvonne Lehman, Tracie Peterson, and many others.

When ordering quantities less than twelve, above titles are $3.25 each.
Not all titles may be available at time of order.

SEND TO: **Heartsong Presents** Reader's Service
P.O. Box 721, Uhrichsville, Ohio 44683

Please send me the items checked above. I am enclosing $ _____
(please add $2.00 to cover postage per order. OH add 6.25% tax. NJ add 6%.). Send check or money order, no cash or C.O.D.s, please.

To place a credit card order, call 1-800-847-8270.

NAME _____

ADDRESS _____

CITY/STATE _____ ZIP_____

HPS 13-02